About the Author

From humble beginnings, being raised in Aberdeen, Scotland, I knew I wanted the world to know what I was capable of. My love of reading sparked my love of writing from an early age. Growing up as a 90s' baby with great works of literature — Harry Potter, Cirque Du Freak, Goosebumps. The dystopian, other worldly fantastics that I'd lose myself in for hours. I want that for the next generation. Something they can lose themselves in. Lockdown led me back to old hobbies and pieces I'd written years before. The inspiration spread back through me and helped me finish this. My first book. I hope this sparks the next generation of writers. That everyone who reads this realises they want the world to know what they are capable of.

CW01391414

About the Author

When a Robin Appears

R. L. Glover

When a Robin Appears

Vanguard Press

VANGUARD PAPERBACK

© Copyright 2023
R. L. Glover

The right of R. L. Glover to be identified as author of
this work has been asserted by her in accordance with the
Copyright, Designs and Patents Act 1988.

All Rights Reserved

No reproduction, copy or transmission of this publication
may be made without written permission.
No paragraph of this publication may be reproduced,
copied or transmitted save with the written permission of the
publisher, or in accordance with the provisions
of the Copyright Act 1956 (as amended).

Any person who commits any unauthorised act in relation to
this publication may be liable to criminal
prosecution and civil claims for damages.

A CIP catalogue record for this title is
available from the British Library.

ISBN 978 1 80016 940 1

This is a work of fiction. Names, characters, businesses, places, events and
incidents are either the product of the author's imagination or used in a
fictitious manner. Any resemblance to actual persons, living or dead, or actual
events is purely coincidental.

*Vanguard Press is an imprint of
Pegasus Elliot Mackenzie Publishers Ltd.*
www.pegasuspublishers.com

First Published in 2023

**Vanguard Press
Sheraton House Castle Park
Cambridge England**

Printed & Bound in Great Britain

This book is dedicated to a lot of important people in my life. First, my Grandad Keith, for never once giving up on me. For telling me when I said I wanted to be a writer, that "'sex sells'" and to just go with it and for also inventing the character of Rodney. I miss you every day. To my Grandpa Bill for encouraging me and telling me to keep at it and not to give up on my dream. To my Auntie Karin for just being a wonderful inspiration to me throughout my entire life. To all my wonderful family and friends (especially the wonderful Chloe, who was the first person to ever read this) for supporting me in every way possible and to my amazing dad who unfortunately won't get to see my finished work. I love you, Dad. To Graham, my wonderful husband who has had to listen to me go on about this idea for years. To Cavern Kingston who gave me the inspiration in the first place with his live streams and podcasts. And lastly, to you, for reading this little idea that started bouncing about my head during the lockdown of 2020.

Chapter One

She laughed as he strummed away at his guitar, lowly singing the comments that people were making in the stream. He was so silly at times, but it felt like she was hanging out with a friend. Oh, and his voice. His voice was silky smooth, like melted chocolate, rich, deep and incredibly yummy.

"I'm gonna have to go now guys. It's been a fun little sing-along today. I'll see you all on Wednesday and remember to make today your best day ever."

The end screen of the stream appeared as Lillian typed in 'bye' and sighed.

"Best day ever? I want an adventure of some sorts," she said to herself as she reached out and gently caressed the screen.

The world around her started to spin and everything blurred around her. Bright flashes of green and purple swirled and danced in her vision as the grey of her living room slowly disappeared. Sparkles whipped through her snowy white curls as she floated less than elegantly through the air. She gently landed with a pop on the floor in a heap. Reaching up, she gently pressed her hand against her temple.

"Erm… Hello?" a silky, smooth, masculine voice, she instantly recognised said from behind her. Lillian jumped in shock and spun around on the spot. A soft gasp graced her lips.

The man before her had thick, luxurious, ebony hair that was ruffled from running his hands through it, flawless, pale skin and a chiselled jaw. His shirt clung to every muscle and she swallowed visibly.

"Nick?" she squeaked, not recognising her own voice.

"I recognise you. Do I know you?" he asked, cocking his head to the side as he looked down at her.

She shook her head.

"Not really?" She looked up at him, her eyes trailing the length of his body. He held out his hand to her and she shivered at the warmth of his skin as she put her hand in his. He smiled at her as he helped her up off the floor. "I don't understand. I was just watching your stream. How am I here?"

He smiled at her again, placing a hand on her lower back and guiding her to the sofa in the corner of the studio. The sofa that she had seen many times before through her tiny computer screen.

"Do you have a name?" Nick asked brushing his dark hair out of his eyes as he sat down next to her. Her heartbeat started to increase at his close proximity and she could tell she was flushed as he looked at her.

"Lillian," she replied, shivering involuntarily as his voice washed over her.

"Lilswood from the stream?" he asked, his eyebrows furrowing with concentration. "Now everything is starting to make sense," he muttered to himself.

She nodded looking down at her hands. "You know my username?" she asked incredulously.

He let out a short laugh. "Of course I do. We talk most nights, whether I'm streaming or not. You're witty and funny and you challenge me. You never miss a stream and you are constantly supporting and encouraging me. There's so many times that I think back over our conversations and overanalyse them. You're always one of the first to comment and give feedback on my videos. I was hoping that you would come to one of the meetups we have planned but this is a lot more… convenient." He smirked as he saw the colour rise in her cheeks. "I must say though, I'm glad you turned up now rather than in five minutes' time. I was away to go take a shower."

She blushed even more as she realised the implications of what he was saying and as she noticed that his black button-up was undone bar two buttons.

"Not that I'm complaining about the present company, but how did I get here? I was at home and now I'm, well, not."

Nick stood up from his seat beside her. "Okay, I think I may know, but first tea?"

She nodded, grateful for some distance from the man in front of her. She found him unbelievably attractive and was just waiting for the moment that she woke up from this dream.

He appeared back in the room, breaking her free from her inner monologue with two cups. "Just milk?" he asked as he handed her the cup.

"Yes, how did you know?" she asked, smiling sweetly in thanks at him.

It was Nick's turn to have the colour flush his alabaster skin. "We spoke about it in a stream once."

She blushed as she raised the cup to her lips, noticing him watching her.

"I'm impressed you remembered," she murmured before taking a warming sip of her tea.

They sat in comfortable silence sipping at their tea for a few moments before Nick started to speak again.

"So, the reason you're here," his voice drifted off. "I'm going to ask you something, it may make me sound pig-headed, but I need to know. You wished for an adventure, right?"

Lillian nodded her head.

"When you wished for an adventure, were you thinking about me?" He reached forward and gently tucked a stray strand of hair behind her ear. Her eyes fluttered closed at the contact.

She swallowed and put her cup down on the table beside her and turned to face him. This couldn't be a dream. He was sitting next to her, had touched her, had made her tea.

"Ah, fuck it," she muttered before responding. "Yes. I was thinking about you."

He leaned back in the chair, his ankle resting on his thigh. "It's a simple answer then, as long as you are willing to believe," he started in his deep, smooth voice. "Do you believe in magic of any sort, Lillian?"

She nodded her head, picking up her cup of tea again and taking a long sip.

"Well, there is such a thing where if two people think about each other at the same moment, touch an object they associate with that person, in our case a computer, and say the same phrase with intent it can make the wish of these people come true. They must have some sort of magical experience for this to occur. Does that make sense?"

She nodded, yet again, her voice suddenly very weak. "You were thinking about me?"

He laughed softly. "I do quite a bit if I'm being honest. What can I say? You intrigue me."

She smiled gently. "So, an adventure?"

He shrugged his muscular shoulders. "I love my life, my music, my channel. I just need something…"

"More," she finished at the same time. His smirk sent her heart racing and she was sure that he would be able to hear it beating against her chest.

"If you're game, why don't we try to establish this magical connection, get to know each other and have some fun at the same time?" he asked, placing a hand gently on her knee.

"I must be dreaming…" she whispered, pinching the back of her hand.

Nick took the cup from her and put it down again, placing a finger gently under her chin to get her to look at him.

"Will this make you realise that this," he indicated between the two of them. "That I am very real."

His eyes were intense. He slowly started to lean forward. When she felt his warm breath, smelling like a mixture of tea and mint, fan across her skin, her eyes fluttered closed. He tipped his head to the side and gently pressed his lips to hers. Her body stiffened for a moment as she let out a startled breath. This was most definitely not a dream and he was kissing her.

Nick's hands moved down to her waist and gently rested there as she relaxed into the kiss and hers wound their way up into his tousled hair. She felt his heartbeat speed up and feeling confident, scooted closer to him until their chests almost touched.

She could have kissed him forever and lived a very happy life but she knew all good things must come to an end. As they separated, she took in his appearance. His hair was dishevelled, and his lips were swollen from her kisses and Lillian thought he had never looked more handsome. She didn't know if he could tell what she was thinking but blushed at the thought of him catching her.

She giggled nervously, picking at the bottom of her dress. Suddenly, she realised what she was wearing. A small, black babydoll dress and knee-high socks, she had been planning on getting changed later, but obviously hadn't expected to be transported across the country and getting kissed silly by the man she'd been dreaming about for months.

His fingertips travelled a slow path along her collar bone. "Enough of an adventure for you?" he whispered into her ear before he ghosted kisses along her neck.

"Never…" she breathlessly replied.

He laughed softly, his hands running up and down her sides, creating goosebumps in their wake.

"I hate to be that person," she said. "But I have to go back or try to figure out how to…"

His face dropped but he quickly schooled it. "Will I see you again? I'm not the sort of person to really do this sort of thing," he asked, suddenly shy.

Slowly, she ran her hands up his arms onto his shoulders and smiled sweetly at him. "If I didn't have to work today, I would happily spend the day and night with you if you wanted." The colour stained her cheeks again as she started to lean forward and gently placed a kiss on his lips.

He smiled into the kiss and muttered against her lips, "We touch the screen at the same time and say 'adventure achieved' and you'll be taken home." He wrapped his arms around her waist and pulled her closer.

"What time do you have to be there?" he asked in a husky voice.

"I have a little while yet," she replied tracing her finger along his jaw. "Although…"

"I don't like the sound of that although," he wrapped his arms around her a little tighter.

She giggled. "All I was meaning was, maybe we should take a little breather and talk a little bit about this magical connection. I must say I am a bit intrigued." She smiled as she picked up her cup and finished drinking her tea.

He chuckled and sat back in the chair, throwing his arm around her shoulders.

"Okay, so I take it you have some experience with magic then?"

He softly ran his fingers across her knuckles of the hand not holding the cup, enjoying the feeling of her hands within his. "A little. I've dabbled in the past. My dad's a warlock, but doesn't really practice any more since we lost my mum. He couldn't find the happiness needed to create any magic, so essentially retired." He leaned over and wiped the tear that had escaped off of her cheek. "What about yourself?" she shakily asked.

"Both my parents are magical. I do the odd bit here and there, but nothing much." He shrugged his shoulders.

"So, I take it you know something about this and have either read or done research about magical connections?" she asked hopefully.

He smiled at her and reached across planting a simple kiss on her cheek. "Sorry, couldn't resist. Yeah, I have a book on it in the other room if you wanted to have a read of it?" Her face lit up and he chuckled. "Oh yeah, English lit nerd." She blushed at his comment.

"You really do pay attention to us, don't you?"

He shrugged again. "If it wasn't for you guys, I wouldn't be in the position to do any of the stuff that I get to do now. I appreciate everything you guys do and all your feedback."

She smiled and traced the pattern of stubble on his chin.

Looking over at the clock, she sighed. "I need to go, Nick, but I promise that I will be back. You aren't getting rid of me that easily."

He held up a finger and dashed to a different room, coming in with a large tome in his hand.

"For you." He bowed slightly as he handed the book over, and blushed as he reached into his back pocket, removing a phone. "Can I get your number so that we can get to know each other and arrange another meet up? Only if you want to that is. I realise you don't really know me and it can be quite intimidating meeting someone online and this has kind of escalated more than I meant to when I first saw you, you were just so beautiful and I couldn't resist you and I wasn't 100 per cent sure it was real myself to start with and now I'm rambling…"

She broke out into a huge smile and placed the hand that wasn't holding the book out for his phone. He gave it to her and she typed in the digits. Lillian handed it back and stepped closer to him. She reached up on her tiptoes and placed a kiss on his lips. He wrapped his arms around her waist and pulled her closer, responding enthusiastically.

"You are adorable. I watch your videos and spend time getting to know you through comments and chats, you think I wouldn't want to know you more. Dude, I have the biggest crush on you, as embarrassing as it is to admit face to face. But I really do have to go…" she whispered, stepping away from him.

Her phone buzzed in her pocket. She took it out and smirked at the message on the screen. "Just making sure that it worked."

She walked over and kissed him again briefly.

Turning back, she grabbed his hand and placed their conjoined hands softly on his computer screen and pressing her body into his whispered, "Adventure achieved." And spun out of the room with a small wave.

She landed in her room a bit more elegantly, managing to stay on her feet this time. She grinned as she looked down at the book in her hand. She threw herself onto her bed, placing the book down and giggling. She had met Nick; they had some sort of connection and he had kissed her more than once. He knew who she was and wanted to continue talking to her.

She snuggled into her pillow, wrapping the blanket around her and picked up the book again.

"I have time for a little bit of reading before work," she murmured, getting comfortable and absorbing herself in the words before her.

Chapter Two

She had been late for work that night. If anyone asked, she would deny it, she was never late for anything. It filled her with a weird sort of anxiety and dread. She was now back home after a fairly uneventful shift. She hated working with fast food, the smell lingered on her for hours until she scrubbed herself with her raspberry and blackberry body wash and matching shampoo and conditioner. She stepped out the shower and wrapped herself in a fluffy black towel and one around her hair.

There was a knock on her front door.

"Just a second," she shouted, making sure that her towel was secure before heading over to find out who was visiting that early on a Monday morning. She was exhausted and rubbed her eyes as she approached the door. One of the downsides of living alone, she had to be the one to answer.

Slowly, she opened the door, toeing on her slippers as she did so. Standing there, with a bright bunch of sunflowers wrapped in an emerald-green bow, was a grinning Nick.

"Morning beautiful," he said handing the flowers to her. She grinned and threw herself at him, enveloping him in a big hug.

"These are lovely," she said, untangling herself from him and sniffing the colourful flowers. "What are you doing here?"

"I wanted to come and see you, take care of you and make sure you rested after work and just to let you know that I had been thinking of you." He stepped into the grey hallway, lined with posters of different horror films. Lillian giggled to herself. It was surreal seeing Nick in her home, dressed in his black ripped jeans, a purple shirt and a leather jacket, a beanie pushing his dark locks out of his eyes.

"I'm afraid that I'm not going to be very good company until I get some sleep. Luckily, last night was my last shift this week, but I need a few hours," Lillian said grabbing his hand and running her fingers across his knuckles. "I'm sorry that you travelled so far for me to need to rest."

He shrugged. "Let's get you to bed then," he said, turning her around and pushing her along the corridor,

"Okay. Okay," she sighed. "Just give me a second. Just head into the room up there and make yourself comfortable." She pointed in the direction of her bedroom.

Lillian ran into the bathroom and closed the door behind her. She let out a breath that she hadn't realised that she had been holding. She looked over at the pyjamas that she had looked out and cursed. There wasn't exactly a lot of material and she would have to walk into the room with

Nick. Hopefully, he wouldn't notice. She put on the tiny shorts and camisole and quickly brushed her hair and teeth.

She took a deep breath before entering her room. She closed the door behind her and turned to see Nick, lounging on her green tartan bedding, a book laid out in front of him. His jacket was laid over the back of her computer chair, his boots tucked away to the side and she couldn't help but smile at the image in front of her.

"If you're finished ogling me, get that cute little butt over here and have a nap." He lifted his head up and visibly swallowed when he looked at her. "Erm, wow."

She blushed, the colour trailing down onto her chest as she walked over to the bed. He pulled up the cover, scooting over to let her get underneath.

"Feel free to make yourself at home, explore the house if you want to. Please don't feel like you need to stay in here," she said, fluffing her pillow up before lying down completely. He slowly got up and moved her cover out of the way so he could lie on the bed beside her, opening his arms, for her to lie cuddled into him.

They both got comfortable and Lillian turned to face Nick.

"Thank you," she whispered as she tilted her head up and ghosted her lips over his. She laid her head down on her arm and fell asleep within a few moments for the most peaceful sleep that she had ever had.

She woke up very much aware of the warm lump that was softly snoring next to her. She turned over onto her side, wriggling ever so slightly to get comfortable again and brush her hair out of her face.

"I'll need you to stop moving like that," Nick said, his voice rough with sleep and his eyes still shut. She giggled and turned to face him.

"Good afternoon," she said, rubbing her hand softly against his cheek, moving his fringe from his eyes.

"Definitely good. I could get used to this," he replied, kissing the crown of her head.

She made a noise of agreement and sat up in the bed. "So, any plans for today then? What adventure would you like to partake in?"

"Mmmmm, I can think of something," he said snuggling in to her waist.

She laughed and yanked the covers off him. "Come on you. Let's go get coffee. I'll quickly get dressed and then we can go… somewhere."

She placed a slow, sensual kiss on his lips, enjoying the feeling of being in control as he slowly sat up. He tried to carry the kiss on, but she slowly got off the bed, giggling as she stepped away from him seeing his pouting face.

She headed to the bathroom and chucked on a black summer dress and some pumps and headed to the kitchen.

Grabbing the two cups of coffee that she had made, two sugars and milk for him, just milk for her, she headed back to her room. She silently kicked the door open and stopped on the spot. Nick was standing there in what he had slept in, just his boxers, with his back to her. She couldn't help but admire the ways his muscles moved as he put on his shirt and slowly buttoned it up. As he bent over to pick up his trousers, she let out a low wolf whistle and he turned around and smirked at her.

"How long have you been there?" he asked, his eyebrow raising along with his question.

She answered his smirk with one of her own, "Long enough. Has anyone ever told you just how handsome you are?" Lillian sauntered over to Nick and handed him his cup of coffee along with a small peck to the cheek.

She took a sip as she leaned against her desk. "So…"

"So?" he countered.

"What you thinking we should do today?" she asked walking over to the window and pulling open the curtains and looking outside at the beautiful sunshine that flooded her garden.

"Why don't we just go outside, spend some more time getting to know each other and we can order takeout tonight and just have a lazy day since you were working all night?"

She couldn't help the smile that broke out on her face. He was so considerate. And it wasn't like she could complain at the company of the sexy man in front of her for the day.

She grabbed his hand, and they walked out into the garden. Nick clicked his fingers and before him lay a checker board picnic blanket and basket.

"Surprise?" he stated.

Shaking her head, she took the blanket from him and laid it down on the grass. Nick threw himself down and she laughed wholeheartedly as she sat down next to him.

"What did I do to be this lucky?" she asked quietly, more to herself than to Nick, but he heard nonetheless and took her hand in his and brought it to his lips and laid a kiss on her knuckles.

She reached up nervously and tucked her hair behind her ear. A dark mark caught the attention of Nick and he scooted closer.

"How long have you had this?" he asked reaching up to push her hair aside.

Her eyebrows furrowed in confusion. "Excuse me?"

He took his phone out of his pocket and took a photo of just behind her ear and flipped the screen round to show her. On her pale skin, there were two little black letters. NM.

"Where the hell did that come from?" she asked looking down at her lap.

He swallowed and muttered "*Revelare particeps,*" as he ran his hand over his wrist, revealing two small characters there. LR.

"Lillian Robertson?" he said and her eyes shot up to his. "I have yours, and you have mine. Nicholas Madden. This all makes sense now." He gathered her up in his arms and started kissing her. First on the lips, then on the cheeks, moving to her neck, before laying her down on the blanket. He stopped kissing her long enough to smile happily at her.

"As much as I'm not complaining," she said between kisses. "What has brought this on? You are going to have to tell me a little bit more." She laughed as he trailed his fingers up her sides, tickling her in the process.

He touched the spot behind her ear and rubbed his finger softly over it. "This has, how much of the book did you read?"

She shrugged. "Only just over a chapter. I was running late," she hated to admit it, but this was Nick she was talking to. She felt like she could tell him anything.

"Okay." He waved his hand and the book was suddenly in front of him. He flipped open to about halfway through and started to read, "A twin flame is an intense soul connection, sometimes called a 'mirror soul',' thought to be a person's other half. It's based on the idea that sometimes one soul gets split into two bodies. One of the main characteristics of a twin flame relationship is that it will be both challenging and healing. This is due to the mirroring nature of a twin flame; they show you your deepest insecurities, fears, and shadows. But they also help you overcome them and vice versa—your twin flame will be equally affected by you." He closed the book with a dramatic flair.

"We're soulmates?" He nodded with a large grin across his face and bent down to kiss her again.

"We were simply meant to be, mon cheri."

"So, the connection brought us together and was the reason I found your stream, the reason we would banter back and forward, etcetera?" she asked, whilst he nodded his head.

He sat up and ran a hand through his hair. Lillian stretched out enjoying the feel of the sun on her skin as her brain swirled with the information that she had just been given. She had thought that her infatuation with him had been for a reason and was more than likely returned.

"Your thoughts are giving me a headache," he said letting out a throaty chuckle.

"Sorry. I'm just processing," she replied.

"Hey." He placed a finger under her chin and tilted it upwards. "I was just kidding." He leaned in and placed a brief kiss on her lips. As he pulled away, he swirled his wrist in a figure of eight motion and his guitar appeared before him. Lillian rolled onto her side and grabbed the book and flicked to the section she had been reading the night before. With Nick's silky smooth voice and light strumming of the guitar, she couldn't feel any more relaxed.

Chapter Three

That night Nick stayed until Lillian could barely keep her eyes open any more. "You can stay if you want. I slept so well this morning," she nervously said, rolling onto her side to look at him with big puppy dog eyes.

Nick laughed, kissed her soundly on the lips and replied, "I wish I could, but I have some things I need to get sorted tonight, but how about a proper date tomorrow night?"

Lillian smiled as she thought about her date, she had fallen asleep happy and woken up even happier. She decided to have a lazy morning once she had awoken and read more about her connection with Nick.

Her head started to spin. She had met her other half, twin flame, the person she was meant to be with. She skimmed over the section that she had been reading yet again. According to an author named Susan Dykes there was three signs to signal that you had met your twin flame:

1. You lived separate lives.

Twin flames often live separate lives. This separateness is essential for knowing yourself at the fullest level prior to meeting the additional half of your soul.

The spiritual growth and path you seek, as well as your determination to clean up your own personal and emotional baggage, is what propels you and your mirror image together. Both of you have to work on yourselves before encountering the other.

When you do encounter each other, the feeling is one of déjà vu. You feel like you've known this person forever, wondering where they have been all of your life. The sparks will fly instantaneously.

At first, you will believe it is all about the physical melding, but time may reveal it is more about the purpose of what you both bring to the table for the good of all, rather than for the good of yourself.

The more internal work you do to clear your insecurities, your selfish ways, even your fears and ego, the closer your twin flame will come towards you. The Universe will draw your energies together without your having to seek or search. Until such time, you may continue to live separate lives.

Lillian sighed. She'd been alone for a long time. Her dad barely had time for her now, she did everything alone and having found Nick, the thought made her smile. She had a person to love and cherish and spend time with. They didn't have to be doing anything. Just sitting in silence together and she would be happy. Maybe that's why they had ended up together. Because she was finally happy with her own company. She gently turned the page to continue on reading.

2. You fight like cats and dogs at first.

When your twin flame arrives, your reunion will have you speaking in terms of feeling, emotion, elation, and curiosity. It will seem as though you both have been on similar paths, though far from each other.

However, there will be times when one of you will deflect deeper evaluations, deeper energy, and deeper emotion than the other is ready to handle. For this reason, one of you may always wish to run.

You will struggle to see yourself in the image of the person in front of you. You may even struggle to admit the change in the face of such depth and perception. The truth is you may not like what you see but your heart will know it as truth.

Hence, arguments like nothing you have ever encountered may ensue.

Your head will tell you to run, to leave, to get the heck out, but your heart will perish just as it did when the mystical god of sky and thunder, Zeus, separated you long ago.

You are mirror images of each other and not everything you see in the mirror is perfect at first.

In the initial stages, you will exhibit a push/pull continuum, one that will possibly leave you raw and vulnerable. Yet, in the end, as time together forges its reconnection, the joining of your souls for the good of all will emerge.

Lillian reread the section again. The section hurt her heart. They were twin flames. it was bound to happen but the thought of fighting with Nick hurt her deeply. She decided to try not to think too much about this as she carried on reading.

3. You feel like each other's home.

When the initial stages of mirror images are complete, you will feel at home in body, mind, spirit, and soul. It will seem as though all of the work each of you has done separately, as well as together has been worth it.

You no longer dread finding the perfect mate, the perfect friend, or the perfect parent—your twin flame will seemingly read your thoughts, your mind, and your body language. Both will be willing to do whatever is necessary to fulfil the purpose of the relationship as one.

Lillian closed the book, her mind going into overdrive. If the book was right, they would have a rocky time coming up, that they would have to work through to get to the connection she had been looking for her entire life.

Lillian's phone buzzed. *Stop overthinking everything... see you soon! N x*

Lillian couldn't help but laugh. She put the book down and climbed out of her bed to head down to the kitchen. She put the kettle on and started to sing a song that had been stuck in her head for a few days now. By the time the kettle had boiled, she was full on dancing round her kitchen. She made her cup of tea and went back to her room to choose what to wear for her date that evening. She had a few hours to spare before she was meeting him and the nerves were slowly starting to build within her.

She decided a nice hot bath would calm her nerves, so went into the bathroom and turned on the hot water. She loved a nice, toasty bath with some sort of aromatic bubbles. As the tub filled up, she sipped on her tea and thought back over the past two days and how everything had changed so rapidly.

As the bubbles reached the top of the tub, Lillian swallowed the last of her tea, placing her cup down on the side, before taking her pyjamas off and sliding into the hot water.

She sighed as the warmth enveloped her and wished that she had a nice book to read to help calm her nerves. As she thought about the book that she was wanting, the air around her seemed to still and suddenly the book appeared at her side. She smiled to herself, it was the first time she had managed to focus on something and it appeared.

As she picked up her book, *Paradise Lost* by John Milton and flicked to the page she had been on, she thought back to when she first found out that she had magical abilities.

She had been six. She had made something float in the classroom and the kids had started to make fun of her, calling her a weirdo and a freak. She was used to this due to the colour of her hair and the fact that it was curly. It had taken her a while to get used to this, but now people's name calling rarely bothered her.

She had run home that night in tears to her mum and dad and they had explained that she was magical, and her dad was a warlock and that eventually she would come fully into her powers. They also showed her how to school her emotions to make sure that her magic didn't escape in front of others. She had been fascinated and had started reading some of her dad's books, but he never had many and it wasn't the sort of thing that you could head to the library and ask for, so her research had stopped.

And then her mother had died. When she asked, her father had sat her down and explained how her mother had been suffering with cancer for a very long time and unfortunately it had finally won the battle. Lillian had cried herself to sleep that night, her magic exploding from her, unable to control it any more. She had tried to speak to her father about it, but he closed himself off, a shell of the man he had once been. Unable to perform any magic himself, unable to work. She couldn't remember the last time she had seen him. It was only really the holidays that she went to visit him.

Lillian sighed as she came out of her daydream. Today was supposed to be a happy day so it wouldn't do to dwell she thought. Her mother would have sat her down and given her a little pep talk. She laughed as she thought about how that would have gone.

She opened her book and decided to reread a section of book one. Satan's soliloquy was always one of her favourite section of *Paradise Lost* to read. It was so interesting to see how Milton had managed to make his character so relatable and make the reader empathise with him.

After reading for a little while and after the water had started to cool, Lillian decided to start the arduous task of getting ready for her date. She started with shaving her legs, then washing her hair and body, before finally getting out of the bath, once all the bubbles were gone.

She wrapped her fluffy towel around her and one around her hair and walked to her bedroom to try and decide what to wear for her date.

Her phone pinged beside her, and she grabbed it, a smile gracing her lips. *Wear something smartish. I've got tonight all planned out. N x*

She laughed as she put her phone down. He always seemed to know what she was thinking, which both worried and excited her at the same time. She was not used to having someone to look after her, she had been doing it by herself for the past five years and now there was someone who wanted to be there for her.

She stood in front of her wardrobe, admiring the many different shades of black. She had no idea what to wear but decided she wasn't going to fret over it too much. She picked out a nice black skater dress with a belt and laid out some tights and picked up a pair of black pumps, she then got to work on her hair. Trying to tame it was almost impossible but she was determined to look her best for tonight.

It took nearly two hours, but she finally felt happy with how she looked. She smiled at her reflection as the doorbell rang. She skipped down the hall, her nerves disappearing as the excitement of seeing Nick took over.

She opened the door, beaming at Nick. "You look beautiful," he said holding up a bouquet of sunflowers with some roses placed in amongst them to her.

"Thank you," she said, spinning around on the spot to show off her outfit. "Is this okay for what you have planned?"

He looked her up and down, obviously checking her out and smiled. "Absolutely perfect. You look stunning," he replied as he swooped in and laid a kiss on her lips.

"You look very handsome yourself," she said looping her arms around his neck and kissing him again. He had his hair slightly tousled, black shirt, smart jeans and his normal leather jacket on.

"As much as I would love to keep this going. We have a reservation we have to keep," Nick said, breaking away from her kisses. He placed the flowers down and laid his hand gently on her back as he guided her out the door.

She quickly locked up before Nick took her hand and lead her to his car.

"Very swish," she said as he opened the passenger door to his 1959 Cadillac sedan Deville.

"It's my baby. I saved up as soon as I started working and knew I wanted to try and get this car. I got it and it needed a little work doing to it, but it now runs beautifully and I love it. I only use it for special occasions however as it is a classic," he rambled on as he got into his seat in the driver side.

"So, this is a special occasion?" Lillian asked smiling as she put her seatbelt on.

Nick reached over and placed his hand on her knee. "Yes, this is a very special occasion," he said.

She smiled to herself as he drove out of her driveway and into the country. They were in the car for a total of twenty-five minutes before he took a turn and headed towards a car park.

When they parked the car, Nick got out and helped Lillian out of her seat.

"This is amazing," she said as she took in the view. They were overlooking the river and could see some breathtaking views of the mountains in the background that had snow covering their peaks. There was a small building to the side of them. "Canadian food?" she asked. She had read about this cafe before and had always wanted to try it but never had the time to.

Nick nodded as Lillian moved towards him, capturing his lips in a searing kiss.

"Thank you," she whispered as they separated and headed towards the door.

"Ah Mr Madden, it's been a while since we last met. Who is this beautiful woman?" the maître d' asked as he shook Nick's hand.

Nick laughed, "This is the lovely Lillian. Lillian, this is Derek, an old friend of mine. He's the one who owns this beautiful establishment."

Lillian shook the hand of the man in front of her. "So, you're the one who got this guy to settle down then?" he said making Lillian laugh.

"Dude…" Nick said, playfully punching his arm.

Derek laughed as they all started walking to a table. He pulled out a seat for Lillian as Nick sat down opposite her.

"Stealing my job," Nick muttered as he picked up a menu and handed one to Lillian. He scowled as he heard Derek laughing as he walked away.

Lillian reached over and grabbed Nick's hand, squeezing it lightly to get his attention.

Nick looked up and smiled hesitantly at her.

"Sorry," he muttered, his hair falling into his eyes.

He looked so handsome and Lillian couldn't resist the urge to scoot her chair closer. She took his face in her hands, gently caressing his cheek and getting him to look with her.

"Hey, hey. I'm here with you, remember that," she whispered before closing the distance between them. This kiss was sweet and tender and only lasted a few minutes, but it was enough to give Nick his confidence back. "Always remember," she said as she took his hand and ran his fingers over his initials on her neck.

Nick smirked at her and scooted just a little bit closer yet again. "I can't help feeling a bit jealous. He always got the girl. I couldn't cope if I lost you too." He kissed her on the cheek, trailing down to where his initials were on her neck.

Derek approached and cleared his throat. "Just a reminder, Mr Madden, that I am indeed married to a very feisty young woman, who would have my balls if I were to even consider cheating on her, so you are completely safe. I promise I will not steal your girl, or I would end up castrated," he said chuckling lightly. "Are you two ready to order or do you want me to get you a room next door?".

36

Lillian started to blush as Nick threw his napkin at Derek who dodged it easily.

Lillian laughed. "I'll have a lemonade, the beef dip and poutine please?"

"Good choice," Derek said jotting it down on his notepad.

"Make it two," Nick said, grabbing her hand and rubbing his thumb across her knuckles. She looked over at him and grinned.

Derek looked between the two of them, nodded his head and walked away.

"So…" Lillian started.

"So?" Nick responded, mocking her slightly.

"Tell me about little Nick?" she said playing with the napkin in front of her.

Nick quirked an eyebrow at her and she started to laugh. "No. Get your mind out of the gutter," she said through her laughter. "Your life growing up I meant."

Nick laughed too, placing his hand on her knee. "Okay, so not a huge amount to know. Dad wasn't around much as he was always at work, mum was the one who brought me up, until a few years ago when we got a maid. She's the one who looks out for me the most. Anyway, everything was pretty normal, we played about with magic a little bit, I went to a school in Scotland and that's basically it." He shrugged his shoulders.

"Sounds nice," Lillian said sadly.

Nick smiled. "I know things weren't always easy for you, but I'm here for you now," he said squeezing her hand affectionately.

She smiled, blinking the tears away. "Thank you," she said trying not to let her emotions get the better of her. "I understand sometimes I'm not the easiest person to know but I appreciate you being here with me anyway."

Derek chose this moment to interrupt them. It was a good job that looks couldn't kill, as the look that Nick gave his friend would have made him drop dead on the spot. He gave them the food and bowed away as Lillian looked on in amazement.

"This looks so good," she said, spreading her napkin over her legs and pulling the plate slightly closer. She closed her eyes and inhaled. Her mouth started to water.

She looked up at Nick who was watching her intently. She picked up her glass stating 'cheers' before clinking glasses with him and taking a sip of her drink.

They ate in comfortable silence, only every now and again stopping to discuss the quality of the food or little bits of information that came into their minds.

Once they were finished, Derek approached with a smile on his face.

"Everything okay for you both?" he asked as he cleared the plates before them. Lillian nodded her head as she gently grabbed hold of Nick's hand.

"It was lovely. Thank you," she said smiling at Derek.

Nick muttered his thanks as Derek walked away. He came back a few moments later. "Can I have the bill please?" Nick asked.

Derek shook his head. "This ones on me bud. It's been far too long since I last saw you and this lovely lady definitely deserved a treat," he said, making Lillian blush.

Nick scowled but thanked him anyway. He helped Lillian out of his chair. "Don't be a stranger," Derek said, seeing them out the building with a wave.

Nick possessively wrapped his arms around Lillian who just giggled. "You are impossible," she said, laughing away to herself. "You know I only want you right?"

"You want me?" he said, quaking his eyebrow at her and trailing his hands up her side.

She playfully slapped his chest. "I didn't mean it like that."

His cheeky grin faltered before Lillian moved closer, wrapping her arms around his waist. "Hey. Of course I want you, in every sense of the word. I just know that if we are meant to be together, there is no need to rush anything. I want to cherish every. Single. Moment," she said punctuating each word with a kiss.

Nick smiled down at her, happily enjoying her company.

"Fancy taking a walk?" he asked, kissing the crown of her head. She nodded grabbing his hand and moving along to the water edge.

"There's something so relaxing about being beside the water," Nick said, staring out into the slowly lapping waves.

They stood there for a while watching the sun setting over the water.

"I'm glad you're here with me," Nick said turning to Lillian.

He dipped his head down and gently slanted his lips over hers. Her lips were soft, plump and warm, if a little chapped from the cold. They moved innocently and gently over his, not moving to deepen the kiss, but not pulling away. He heard a soft, contented sigh, and the noise tipped him over the edge. He traced his tongue over her lower lip as he had wanted to earlier, and she immediately parted for him. He could feel himself becoming dizzy with his growing desire for her.

Slowly they separated and Lillian shivered.

"Let's get you home," he said as he wrapped his arm around her shoulder.

"I've had a lovely evening, Nick. Thank you so much for tonight," she said as they walked to the car.

He smiled breathtakingly at her and she couldn't catch her breath.

"No problem. I'm glad. Sorry for being jealous earlier," he started.

Lillian laughed gently. "Don't worry. It was kind of sweet."

They headed back towards the car and Nick drove Lillian home. She spent the entire time looking out of the window.

"Thank you so much," she said as Nick opened the door for her. He caught her hand and kissed her knuckles gently as he walked her to her door.

"I'm not ready for this to end," she said sadly.

"Who says it has to end? If you're up to it, let's just go inside and talk and maybe some more of this…" he said, as he leaned towards her and stole another sublime kiss. Her hands made their way into his soft tresses, her fingers gentle as they weaved through the hair at his temples.

They separated and Lillian unlocked the door.

"Well, in you come then," she said, stepping aside and he walked in, shutting the door behind her, hoping to get to know each other better as the night continued.

Chapter Four

"I have someone that I think you should meet," Nick said a few days later as Lillian and he lay in bed. She rubbed her eyes, it had been a long night at work the previous night, but knowing that Nick would be there the next morning made everything a little better.

"Okay, do I have to be overly presentable, or can I be comfy for meeting the person?" she asked snuggling into his side a little bit more, wrapping the covers up over her shoulders.

"You can be as comfy as you like," he said, placing a gentle kiss on the crown of her head.

She sighed happily. "So it's not your parents then or something like that?"

He laughed as he slowly sat up in bed. "Nah, unless you want to, that is," he said laughing at the expression on her face.

"I'm good just now," she laughed, sitting up beside him and stretching her arms out above her head. "Let me get dressed and you can tell me who we are going to see on the way there."

She got up and skipped to the bathroom, going for a shower before getting ready. She took her time washing her hair and her body before getting out and drying herself thoroughly whilst singing away to herself. She chucked on some leggings and an oversized jumper before tying her wet hair up into a bun on top of her head.

She walked through to the bedroom, still singing and Nick came and grabbed her hand, dancing and singing along with her. She giggled away as they playfully danced around her room.

Eventually, they separated and finished getting ready before Nick took her over to the computer. "You remember the phrase?" he asked as he grabbed her hand and placed it gently on the computer.

She nodded her head and they both said, "I want an adventure."

The world around them began to spin and colours of purple and green spun around them. They landed with a pop in a room that looked like an office. Lillian's eyes widened as she looked around her.

"This is incredible!" she exclaimed as she saw the rows upon rows of books before her. "Where are we?"

Nick laughed at her reaction. "You are adorable but very predictable," he said as he moved towards a desk in the corner of the room. Lillian followed just behind him and took a seat beside him.

"Do you think I'll be allowed to have a look around?" Lillian asked, making Nick belly laugh.

"Stop being so cute," he said kissing her quickly on the lips, making her blush.

A door opened behind them and footsteps approached. "Nick, my boy, how are you? It's been a while," an older gentleman, with a beard as white as snow and round glasses that framed his twinkling azure eyes, said as he came over to shake Nick's hand. "Who is this lovely lady?"

"Julius, this is Lillian. Lillian, this is Julius. He has tutored and helped me with my magic throughout my entire life. I thought that maybe he could help you too," Nick said as Lillian and Julius shook hands.

"So twin flames?" he asked, his eyes sparkling with amusement. Lillian blushed as she nodded her head.

"How interesting, I had a friend named Rodney, who met his soulmate. They weren't twin flames but they were perfectly matched. She was a Newar from the Kathmandu Valley. Very pretty girl, although I never did understand the whole bone through the nose thing. He never did let it go how he'd met his soulmate… sorry I went off on a tangent," he said sitting down opposite Nick and Lillian.

Nick was grinning as Lillian looked around the room at all the books.

"Definitely a Robertson," he muttered to himself. "My dear, if you want to have a look, feel free. There's books in here from all around the world, every language, covering every religion, every form of magic that is known. If there is anything in particular that you are interested in, just let me know," Julius said looking down at his notebook. "I have a photographic memory so know where everything is. Oh, where are my manners," he said startling Lillian from her time perusing the books. "Tea? Same us usual, Nick? Lillian, let me guess, just milk?"

Lillian nodded her head and watched the older gentleman leave the room.

"How does he do that?" she asked Nick as she approached him with a book in her hand.

Nick shrugged. "Just very intuitive, I guess. He's always been like that. I've known him as long as I can remember. I'm pretty sure when I was younger, I spent more time with him than I did with my own father."

Lillian pecked Nick on the cheek and went to sit down on the window seat. The sun was shining in through the bay window and she couldn't help but bask in the sun. The feeling of warmth and brightness was comforting to her.

Julius walked in and chuckled to himself. "Of course that's where you would sit. It was the same seat she would always choose. You really are the double of your mother, my dear."

Lillian looked up from her book at a smiling Julius, who had her tea in his hand.

"You knew my mother?" she asked, taking it from him, embracing the warmth of the cup.

"I know a lot of people, my dear. I have worked on every continent in this world at some point or another in my long life. I was in the navy at one point, you know? Your mother is a very lovely person, who by the looks of it has raised a brilliant child," Julius said, taking his seat again.

"I'm sorry to tell you but my mother passed away. She had a fight with cancer when I was younger," Lillian quietly said, taking a sip of her tea.

"Oh, my dear. I'm so sorry you had to go through that. No child should ever have to deal with the loss of a parent that young. You should always have them with you. Have you tried to contact her? No one is ever truly gone, especially if they have unfinished business on this plane, which I'm assuming your mother did."

Lillian looked quizzically at Julius and then at Nick. Nick smiled at her empathetically and mouthed the words, 'you okay'? at her. She slowly nodded her head, looking down at her cup. She slowly traced the astrological pattern that adorned the cup.

They sat quietly for a while, Lillian and Julius each reading, sipping their tea in the process and Nick looking at the different titles that adorned the many shelves.

Lillian looked at the same page that she had read several times and sighed. She started to bite her nails nervously, looking to see if she could catch Nick's attention. She felt bad that she felt this way as Julius seemed so lovely and she didn't want to offend him. However, all this information about her mother was enough to make her feel a little uneasy and she needed time to process everything that he had said.

"Julius, I'm not feeling too well. Im sorry to break this meeting up so early. It has been very informative and it was lovely to meet you. Is there any chance I could borrow this book? I'll make sure you get it back as soon as I'm finished reading it," Lillian asked.

Julius approached, picked up the book and looked at the cover. "*Necromancy*. Interesting… of course you can. If you wish, I can tutor you on how to refine your magic and we can focus on this during our lessons too? Just like I did with Nick when he was a young boy, although never on this topic. It is up to you however," he said as he handed the book back to Lillian. She smiled at him thankfully.

Nick and Lillian finished their tea before they started heading toward the computer in the centre of the room. "Oh, and Lillian, I really am sorry about your mother. She is an amazing woman, always was and always will be. Reach out to her, I'm sure she'll appreciate it," he said, taking a seat again.

Nick looked at Lillian, wrapped his free arm around her waist and nodded and they both said 'Adventure achieved', spinning out the room together in a flurry of colour.

Julius watched and chuckled to himself, going back to writing in his journal. *Today, I met Lillian Robertson. She is exactly like her mother… I can't wait to see where this goes.*

He put down his pen and smiled to himself as he sipped at his tea, the steam fogging up his glasses.

When Lillian and Nick got back to her house, she collapsed into a fit of tears. "I'm so sorry," she sobbed. "I just didn't expect him to bring up my mother. I miss her so much. Sometimes I just want to talk to her so badly that it hurts. There is so much that I don't know about her."

Nick collected her in his arms and kissed her gently on the forehead.

"Sssh, it's okay. I'm here for you," he said gently rubbing her back. "I'll always be here for you."

She cuddled into him, sighing happily as he wiped her tears from her face.

"Thank you," she whispered before she fell into an uneasy sleep, her head lying on Nick's knee. He picked up her *Necromancy* book and started to read, intrigued in what she would be learning, thinking it was something new he would like to try too. There was a couple of people he knew he would like some answers from and maybe this was the way to find out what was going on. Life was certainly changing, and he was getting the adventure he had desired, he just hoped that it would end happily, but had a feeling in his stomach that something was away to happen. He just wasn't sure what.

Chapter Five

"So." Lillian skipped over and plopped herself down on the sofa next to Nick. They had been going between each other's houses for a couple of weeks now, getting to know each other, flirting and a lot of affection, which Lillian wasn't used to.

"When am I going to get to try this fabulous cooking that you are constantly telling us about?" She crossed her legs in front of her and picked up the extra controller from the coffee table. She felt so at home spending time in his house, that it had been several days since she had been home.

"Erm, excuse me? Who said you could play? Sabotage!" he shouted as Lillian grabbed the controller from his hands, hiding it behind her back.

Her stomach hurt so much from laughing at his shocked expression. He looped his arms around her waist and started to tickle her. The tears streamed down her face as she laughed uncontrollably.

"I surrender," she cried out through giggles. He stopped tickling her and his face grew serious as he pulled her into his lap. His gaze was intense and his hand lifted from its place on her hip to tunnel into her hair. His hand cupped the back of her head as they both leaned forward.

His lips brushed over hers tentatively and her hands ran up his arms to his shoulders of their own volition. His lips were warm and his breath tasted like the coffee that he had been drinking. Her cheeks flushed in pleasure and she nipped at his lips.

He chuckled as they separated. "Why can't I control myself around you?" he asked, resting his forehead against hers.

Lillian kept her eyes closed and sighed contently, burrowing her face into his neck.

"So, food?" he asked, keeping her close but grabbing the controller from behind her so they could play the game together.

"Mmm, yeah. I mean, you have done several streams, cooking delicious looking food, so I would love to try some it someday. I am a little bit sick of take away food," she replied, hammering the buttons on the controller, chuckling as she saw Nick's face…

"Wait. How did you get so good at this?" he asked, trying desperately to win back his advantage.

She shrugged her shoulders and giggled. "Never underestimate me," she said, kicking her feet up over his lap and lying backwards slightly, her head propped up on a pillow as she killed three characters in the game, including Nick's in the process.

"Hey…"

She laughed. "Don't sulk! Loser makes dinner, deal?"

He shook his head, smirking as he picked up the other controller. "Deal. Bring it on!"

The game didn't last long. Five minutes thirty-four seconds to be precise. She jumped up onto the coffee table and started doing a ridiculous dance. She blushed when she realised what she had done, but Nick shrugged it off, wrapping his arms around her waist, lifting her up and spinning her round. "You are adorable," he stated, gently brushing her lips with his. "But I suppose I better get set up in the kitchen. A bet is a bet after all."

Whilst he pottered about in the kitchen, she curled up on the sofa with one of Nick's books on elemental magic. She had started reading the book she had got on *Necromancy* but that needed a lot of concentration, and she just wanted a bit of light reading for now. She focused on the air in front of her and raised her left hand, palm facing upwards.

"*Meridiem*," she whispered, feeling a rush of wind wrap around her as the air changed to a bright yellow light that danced around her.

A huge smile broke out on her face and trying to keep her excitement in place, she walked through to the kitchen, all her energy focused on what she had achieved.

"What's all this?" she said happily looking around at the kitchen. She lost her concentration and the yellow light burst from her. There were candles all around the room, his filming equipment set up and the table set for two with deep red roses and sunflowers in the centre. The table was set with a black lace tablecloth and Nick was dressed in a black shirt and ripped jeans. "I had an idea, if you are up for it? But first, that was amazing? Air magic?"

She nodded her head happily, still taking in the sight in front of her.

"I don't know if you realise it, but you managed to combine your air magic with fire magic. None of these candles were lit before you came into the room. It is very impressive, the fact that you managed to control it in such a way that the whole room didn't go up in flames. It's fascinating as fire and air have contradictory qualities. Fire is both hot and dry, whereas air is hot and wet. Normally when people manage to perform elemental magic, it's one of the elements that they conquer, not two. This is fascinating."

Her jaw went slack. "I wasn't really trying to do that, just trying to keep the light glowing. I, I, I just wanted to show you."

He walked over to her and wrapped his arms around her waist.

"It must just all be raw, natural talent then." He kissed her cheek. "Don't look so worried. We can practice and make sure you know how to control it. Worst comes to worst, we can ask my parents about it. They might have a better understanding of it all than us."

She nodded her head again, wrapping her arms around his neck. She was feeling drained. She wasn't sure if it was from the magic or all the information that she had just been given. Her brain had gone into overdrive, and she wanted to find as many books as possible on elemental magic that she could, to gain information on it.

"Hey." He pressed his lips to the crown of her head. "Let me get you a drink." He walked her over to a chair, pulling it out for her and heading to the fridge to get her a glass of water. "So, my plan?" Nick had a smirk on his face and she couldn't help but smile as she took the glass from him. She took a mouthful and looked at him, waiting for him to continue. "Well, how about we collaborate and make dinner together but stream it. Everyone knows you from the chat and I don't want to hide you. I thought it might be nice. I want them to know how happy you make me."

Red stained his cheeks as he looked at her hopefully. She couldn't resist. As much as the thought of appearing on one of his videos filled her with anxiety, but he looked so happy and had gone to so much effort in preparing she couldn't have said no even if she had wanted to.

"Let me get changed first. You look all handsome and I'm currently in one of your shirts." She laughed, thinking of some of the shocked reactions of his followers. "Give me an hour."

"But I like you in my shirts," he started before she stood up and kissed him soundly on the lips.

She giggled as she bolted out of the room and ran up the stairs straight into the bathroom. She grabbed some bobby pins and carefully pinned her white curls up, leaving a few strands cascading down framing her face. She applied her normal make-up, a little foundation, thick winged eyeliner and a nude lipstick. She stood in front of the full-length mirror and removed the shirt that she had been wearing. She stood in her black underwear and looked at her reflection. She contemplated what she would wear, thinking hard about a black, skin-tight dress with scalloped neckline and a pair of black patent heels. She felt a tingle wash all over her skin and looked on amazed as the outfit that she was currently thinking of appeared on her body. She was in awe of how pretty she looked and the fact that it had actually worked.

Slowly, she made her way down the stairs, holding gently on to the banister.

As she approached the bottom few steps, she saw Nick come over and she smiled her best dazzling smile at him. He bowed slightly and held out his hand for her. She placed her hand lightly in his and he tucked it into the crook of his elbow. He walked her to the kitchen and spun her round in his arms. He flicked his wrist and some romantic music started to play in the background. Taking one of her hands in his and laying the other on her hip, she loosely wrapped her arms around his neck as they started to dance.

"You ready for this?" he whispered into her ear. "Once we go public, there is no going back."

"I never in my wildest fantasies thought that this could ever happen. I'm more than ready to make whatever this is public. I mean, we've never really discussed it apart from the fact that we're soul bound. We kind of just accepted it and let whatever happened happen," she said, running her hand up to cup his cheek. He leaned into her slightly. "And I'm more than okay with that," she added quickly.

"Well, do you want to have that chat?" he asked, still pressing his cheek against her hand.

She softly placed her lips against his neck, murmuring into the skin, "It can wait." They continued their dancing.

After a few minutes, he spun her again and bowed slightly. "I hate to stop this right now, but I believe we have a stream waiting for us."

He walked her over to the seat that he had prepared earlier and pulled it out for her. He smiled mischievously as he pressed the button on the camera and loaded up the laptop. She took a deep breath and looked down at her hands as the countdown timer started.

"Hey guys, gals, non-binary pals. I'm very lucky today to be joined by one of your lovely lot. Everyone give some love to Lilswood." Lillian waved at the camera shyly. "We thought we would just do a quick stream tonight and do a little cooking."

"Time for one of us to find out if this man can actually cook," she added laughing as she elbowed him in the ribs.

Lilswood, you look beautiful.

What a beautiful smile you have.

That dress is stunning, jealous.

The lovely comments flooded the stream and Lillian couldn't help but blush.

Nick started cooking and talking away to the chat as Lillian sat mesmerised. She couldn't help the smile that appeared on her face and no matter how hard she tried she couldn't shift it.

Every now and again she would glance at the comments and either respond or tell Nick what was being said.

"Come on then Lil, I'm gonna need a hand with this part," Nick said, offering his hand to her. She grabbed it and walked with him to where he was preparing food.

Such a gentleman (several love heart emojis).

Look at the way they are looking at each other.

Do I see one of us succeeding in getting Nick's heart?

The comments made her blush and she tried to focus on the feeling of his hand on hers instead.

"So, what toppings do you want on your pizza?" he asked, pointing to the bases that he had been preparing.

"I can't believe you made this from scratch?" she replied, grinning.

She reached over and grabbed some cheese, sprinkling it over the base and then some ham, mushrooms and chicken. She spread the pieces out evenly and put mozzarella slices on the top. Nick grabbed the camera and zoomed in on her working, his smile noticeable from behind the camera.

"Check her out. She's a pro!" he said in a sing-song voice.

She laughed. "Hate to break it to you but I used to work in a pizza restaurant."

We don't need to check her out, you're doing plenty of that (winky face).

Nick's doing plenty of checking out for us. Do you blame him? She's beautiful.

Lillian didn't read the comments, she preferred just having the natural conversation with Nick and leaving him to talk to the people who had joined them. It was his stream after all, and she felt like she was interrupting.

She grabbed both the pizzas and headed towards the oven with them. She placed them on the wire rack and went and sat next to Nick.

"So, I'm sure you are all wondering how I managed to get the lovely Lillian to join me tonight." He grabbed hold of her hand at this point. "Well, I wanted you guys to be the first to know. Lillian is really special to me and I'm hoping that she likes me enough to maybe be my girlfriend?"

Say yes!

She'd be silly to decline.

Lucky girl. The way he's been looking at her all night. Never mind the pizza, it looks like he wants to eat her.

She blushed and looked at him, he was smiling at her with so much adoration she knew her answer straight away.

"Yes," she said, and he reached over, placing a hand on each cheek and kissed her soundly.

The screen filled with love heart emojis and Lillian blushed when they pulled apart and looked at the screen. The timer dinged in the background, so Lillian walked over and took the pizzas out the oven, thankful for the interruption from the comments on the screen. She laid them down on the side as Nick came over with the camera and took a zoomed in shot of the food completed. He turned the camera round and wrapped his arm around her shoulders.

"Well, everyone. Time for my amazing girlfriend and I to enjoy these yummy pizzas. See you next time and remember to…"

"Make today your best day ever," Lillian finished for him. He sent her a breathtaking smile as he turned off the stream. "Well, that was a ridiculously large display of affection."

"You said that you wanted the conversation. Everyone was asking and I was kind of getting a little bit jealous of all the comments that were being made in the chat. I wanted to make sure that they realised you were mine." He grabbed her hands and started rubbing circles on the back of her knuckles, leaning in to place a gentle kiss on her lips.

"As much as I would love to continue this," she said, biting his lip softly. "That pizza smells amazing and I'm starving."

She danced past him to where the pizza was and sliced both of them into multiple pieces. She plated them up and walked over, handing Nick his food. She took a bite and moaned with how good it tasted.

"Okay, you win. Your cooking is amazing," she sighed, licking her lips.

Nick reached out and grabbed her hand. "I mean it, I might have been jealous, but I really do like you and want to see where this goes. The soul bond thing aside. You mean a lot to me already and it's just been a few weeks."

Lillian blushed.

"I'd like that too," she said smiling brightly.

"So, you'll be my girlfriend? I know I shouldn't have asked you on the stream and I got a bit caught up in the moment, but I really did mean it," he babbled on.

Lillian laughed, "Of course I will."

She looked up at Nick and the look in his eye was intense. His lips quirked up into a small smile and he slowly moved forward, capturing her lips.

Lillian lost herself to the taste of him, the feel of his lips on hers. She sighed as his hands cupped her face, holding her as he deepened the kiss, stealing what little breath she had. Eventually, they pulled apart panting, the need for oxygen outweighing their desire for each other.

"Mine?" he whispered, his breath ghosting her lips as he moved down to kiss his initials behind her ear.

"Yours," she responded, reaching for his hand and entwining their fingers. She sighed happily as they moved from the kitchen back to the living room. As they sat down, he handed her a controller and tucked a blanket over both of their legs as they got comfy to play some video games. It was the perfect evening.

Chapter Six

Lillian sat at the other side of the room watching him in his element. She snuggled down under the tartan blanket, feeling the warmth envelop her as she read the book that was spread open on her lap. A book on potions and the effect that they have on the human body and the mind, that currently couldn't captivate her attention as much as the man at the other side of the room.

This had become their routine. Lillian would head home to work Friday, Saturday and Sunday nights, when Nick would stay at her place and the rest of the week they would stay at his, getting to know each other. She could feel herself falling for him, but it had only been a few weeks so she didn't want to ruin anything by telling him of her feelings too soon.

Nick caught her eye as he looked up from the computer screen and smiled. He laughed at something that someone had written to him on the chat and started off on another story, another tangent, as she listened to his warm, calming tone.

She felt the tingle of his magic reach for her and wrap her in a comfortable embrace. She giggled and focused on sending her magic back to him, concentrating on all her feelings for him and how happy she was. He shuddered as the force of her magic washed over him. Her magic was getting more powerful and she was able to focus it more with each day that she practised.

Nick laughed at a comment that appeared on the screen as he strummed his guitar.

"So, guys, I have some news actually. Who's ready to hear my new EP? I've been working on something and I want you all to be the first to hear it."

Lillian looked up from her spot at the opposite side of the room. He hadn't told her about anything like this. She quirked an eyebrow at him, and he shrugged in her direction. She grabbed her phone and logged in to the chat to see what people were saying.

"For the first time in a long time, I've felt motivated to write and play and I thought why not write what I'm feeling," he responded to some comments.

So does that mean it's about Lilswood?

Has she heard the song yet?

Is there going to be a music video to go with the song?

"Whoa! Hold your horses. No, she hasn't heard it. There will be a music video and you can make your own judgement once you've heard it."

He started to strum a beautiful melody on his guitar, his hair falling over his eyes as he concentrated on the tune that came forth from his fingers and the strings. She couldn't take her eyes off of him.

"You appeared right in front of my eyes,
Like a twist of fate,
An angel fallen in disguise,
Are you a mirage?
Appearing amidst a drought?
Feel like I'm drowning,
Felt like the world was coming to an end,
But now I'm not afraid,
My sanity has been saved,
My angel fallen from above,
No more drowning in my tears,
Being drawn in by the flame,
I see the passion in your eyes,
I feel the tenderness of your touch,
I taste the emotion on your lips,
And you're forever in my heart,
Gluing the pieces one by one,
Fixing all the broken parts of me,
My saving grace fallen from above,
My angel in disguise."

Nick finished strumming with an elegant crescendo at the end and placed his guitar down to the side. He raked a hand through his hair and blushed as he looked up at Lillian and then at the screen. Lillian hadn't been able to look away from him during the entire performance. She focused all her energy on the cushion that was beside her and hurled it across the room at Nick. It hit him square in the face, shocking him in the process.

Is that Lilswood? Can we see her reaction?

What did she think?

Lils' reaction on camera please? We assume that it was about her? Lucky girl…

Nick looked up to see Lillian's magic visibly fizzing around her. He swallowed and looked towards the camera. "Guys, gals and non-binary pals, I'm going to have to go. Hope you have a good one and remember to make today your best day ever."

As Nick was ending the stream, Lillian saw the comments that were coming in and rolled her eyes.

He's totally getting laid for that song.

She is such a lucky girl.

I would do anything to be in Lils' shoes. Jealous isn't even the word.

He crossed the room to Lillian as she launched her phone across the floor. "They are a bunch of thirsty bitches…" she muttered as he threw himself into the seat next to her.

"Is there a reason I got attacked with a cushion?" he asked, snuggling into her side.

"One. You never told me you were writing any music. Two, I take it they are right and that it is about me?" Nick nodded his head. "Three. Appearing amidst a drought? Having a dry spell? Oh, and suddenly I appear and poof, the dry spell is over… Wow, way to make me feel cheap," she said, angrily pushing him away. She stood up, slamming her book down on the table and stormed out of the room. "Oh, and you might have to have a word with those girls about boundaries…"

She headed to the bathroom, locking the door behind her. She ran the hot water of the bath, adding a different concoction of fragrances and bubbles. As the steamy water filled the tub, she slowly peeled her clothes off and lowered herself into the bubbles.

Only a few minutes passed before there was a knock at the door which Lillian ignored and sank further into the water so that the bubbles were up to her shoulders.

She swished her wrist and muttered, "Fabula." Soft music began to fill the room.

She heard the door unlock from the outside and watched as Nick came in and removed his clothes. She closed her eyes so that she wasn't tempted to ogle him as he stripped before her. He slowly slid in the bath behind her.

"Bloody hell woman! Are you trying to burn your skin off?" he hissed as his skin started to turn red. He pushed her hair away from the skin of her neck and placed a stray kiss there. "I'm sorry Lils. I promise you that I did not mean the lyrics that way. The way I meant them was that I was feeling empty inside before I met you and now, there are so many emotions and feelings and I'm starting to feel whole again and that is all down to you. I'm sorry if it came across any other way but I really did mean it as someone who cared deeply for the other. We haven't even had sex yet, I mean this is as intimate as we've been. Not that I mind waiting, but if it was about that, then I'd be a jerk for broadcasting it for everyone to hear. If I ever feel inspired to write something about us being together in such a way, I promise, it will be for you and your ears only."

Lillian turned her head round and caught his lips in a soft kiss. "I'm sorry. I overreacted. The song was beautiful and I really appreciate the fact that you wrote it for me."

Nick grabbed some of the shower gel from the side of the bath and rubbed it into the skin of her shoulders. She let out a moan as all the strain and anxiety of the day melted from her.

"You are far too good at that," she said giggling as his fingers trailed across her skin.

Her hands rubbed up and down his legs as he laid gentle kisses on her shoulders and neck.

"Hmm, Nick?" Lillian murmured as his kisses continued to trail down her neck and along her shoulders.

"Yes?" he whispered into her skin.

"I think you're going to have to stop," she said huskily as his lips slowly came up off her skin.

He looked confused as she slowly slipped out of the bath, his eyes watching her every curve. She grabbed a towel and wrapped it around herself before holding out her hand to him.

"Are you going to make me finish off what you started by myself?" she said giggling as her hips wiggled from side to side as she walked. She looked back over her shoulder as she got to the door. "You coming?" She winked at Nick as he scrambled to get out the bath, grabbing a towel and following his sexy girlfriend out of the room.

Chapter Seven

"Come on Nick. Stop it, I need to get ready," she said, turning around in his arms as he continued to kiss her neck, gently nibbling on the skin, making her moan. "Nick, we are going to be late!" she said giving in to the sensations he was causing. She cupped his cheek and brought his lips firmly to hers. "Okay, just five more minutes then," she said as she ran her hands up his chest, raking her nails along his bare flesh. His shirt hung open and his hair was in disarray, evidence from their activities of the last forty-eight hours.

Lillian moaned and caught his mouth with her own. He tasted like heaven. All dark and smooth, like chocolate. He was going to her head like a shot of fine whisky, . She whimpered a little as he sucked on her tongue. And just like that, he pulled away.

"W-Why did you pull away?" she demanded, still dazed from the kiss.

He couldn't help the tiny twitch that curled the corners of his mouth upward at hearing her complain. "My dear, I believe it is your friends that we are going to be late to meet." He winked at her. "However, we can continue this later if you so desire."

She closed her eyes and hummed in agreement. "You're right. I'll go get showered and dressed." She sighed, turning to face him yet again. "Unless I can convince you to join me?" She giggled as she skipped away to the bathroom.

As she dried her hair after a very long and not very cleansing shower, she couldn't help the smile that spread over her entire face. She had forced Nick to go to a different room to get ready so that she wouldn't be distracted. She piled her hair on top of her head, slowly curling the section that she had left hanging down. As she continued to style her hair she thought back over the last few weeks. Things had moved very quickly, but she was so happy. Everything was working in her favour; she had the man she had wanted for a long time and he wanted her back. He was the definition of handsome but also had the personality to go with it.

She smiled to herself as she thought about Nick waiting for her in the other room. She dropped her towel and slid the dress she was planning on wearing over her head and pulled it down. She admired it as she zipped her boots up and did a twirl in front of the mirror. She walked slowly towards the door and headed down to the living room where Nick was waiting for her.

She walked in and stopped to look Nick over. His hair was still wet and laid in natural curls, a plaid shirt moulded to the shape of him, rolled up the elbows and his black ripped jeans. He looked amazing, hunched over his guitar, slowly strumming away.

Lillian cleared her throat as she approached him, wrapping her arms around his neck to place a gentle kiss on his cheek.

"Ready handsome?" she asked as she helped pull him up off of the sofa.

"Lillian, wow… You look stunning," he said, stuttering over his words, she blushed at his compliment.

"Ready to go?" she asked, changing the subject.

"Do we have to?" he said, placing several kisses along her neck.

"Yeah, but we will be back in a few hours," she said, taking his hand in hers.

He groaned as she pulled him along. "Come on. I promise they won't bite."

They took a taxi to the restaurant that they were meeting Lillian's friends at. She took his hand as they headed inside *The Sacrament* and headed toward a table for four that had been booked for them. The inside of the restaurant was beautiful, it was very cosy and was decorated with red and black velvets. Each table was lit with pillar candles and had multiple shades of red roses in the centre.

"This is great," Nick said, looking around, his eyes wide with wonder at the venue. "This would be a fantastic setting for a music video." He spun around looking at the artwork that adorned every wall and each table as they walked past.

As they reached their table, Nick stopped to pull out Lillian's chair for her.

"Derek isn't here to steal my chance away this time," he said as he kissed her cheek.

"Aw, isn't that the cutest thing that I have ever seen," a voice from behind them said excitedly. Lillian turned around to see the beaming smile of her friend.

"Ruby!" she exclaimed excitedly, getting up from her chair and running to give her friend a hug.

"Ruby, this is Nick. Nick, this is Ruby, my best friend from the hell hole I call work," she said laughing as Ruby ran over and hugged Nick, much to his shocked expression.

"Lovely to meet you," he said, laughing gently as he untangled himself from the bubbly girl in front of him,

They took a seat as they waited for the fourth member of their party to join them. After about five minutes, two girls sauntered over to them, waving as they approached.

"Hey Lillian, Ruby, I hope you don't mind that I invited Scarlet," the leggy brunette said as she pulled a fifth seat over to the table. She stuck her hand out to Nick.

"Hi Nick, I've heard so much about you. I'm Izzie and this is Scarlet. We both work with Lillian too." Nick shook both of their hands and poured them all a glass of water as they all looked over the menus in front of them.

Lillian looked up and noticed Scarlet's eyes were trained on Nick. She scowled momentarily. Nick looked up and saw the expression on Lillian's face.

"You okay?" he whispered, softly squeezing her knee. Lillian smiled, the smile not quite reaching her eyes and nodded her head.

The waiter appeared and took everyone's orders before hustling away to deal with other tables.

"So, Nick. We've heard lots about you, but not about how you two met. Care to share your story?" Ruby said, winking at Lillian.

Lillian groaned, but Nick smiled and started talking. "It's not a very interesting story to be honest. We met at a venue when I was playing a gig and then we started talking online and as they say, the rest is history," Nick said, smiling affectionately at Lillian who mouthed 'thank you' at him. Lillian smiled at Ruby and the other girls as they all fell into a natural chatter. Every time Lillian looked up, she noticed that Scarlet was staring at Nick.

The waiter came over and started to hand out the food that everyone had ordered. Lillian looked down at the steak that was in front of her and couldn't wait to dig in. She had a healthy appetite, she knew. She wasn't like Scarlet and Ruby, who were both all long legs, curves and boobs and had beautiful flowing hair. Gorgeous, no other word for it. She sighed as she looked at Scarlet with her salad and Ruby with her soup and suddenly felt very self-conscious about her decision of food.

She sat and picked at her food, ignoring the conversation going on around her. Nick tried to get her attention several times, but her eyes never left her plate. The meal passed quickly and before they all knew it, it was time to go dancing.

Nick took Lillian's hand as they walked the small distance to the club. He paid for her entry and they walked in together. The music was loud and thumped off the walls. He smiled as he did a silly little dance to try and make her giggle.

"You okay?" he shouted, to make sure she could hear him over the music.

She nodded as he grabbed her waist and started to dance to the music. He continued trying to help her loosen up, but nothing was working.

"Two secs," she said, holding up two fingers as she pointed towards the bathrooms.

She walked over to the sink and splashed some water on her face and took a deep breath. "Can you believe he's actually with her?"

Lillian hurried into the cubicle, as she heard Scarlet and Izzie.

"Actually yes. Lils is lovely. Why wouldn't he be with her?" Izzie asked as they approached the sinks.

Scarlet reapplied her lipstick and smirked. "He won't be by the end of the night, especially if I have my way."

"You are awful," Izzie said giggling as they walked out the toilets together.

Lillian walked out the cubicle, trying not to get emotional. Nick was hers and had made it very clear since the day that they first met that he liked her. She took a couple of deep breaths and headed back outside to find Nick.

She walked through the crowded club, bumping into several people on the way. As she approached nearer where she had left Nick, she stopped dead in her tracks, Scarlet was dancing with him in what could only be described as an obscene manner, she was grinding against him and giggling, trying to land kisses on his neck and cheek.

Lillian stormed past them on the way to the bar, intentionally knocking into Scarlet but unfortunately sending her into Nick's arms.

"Bitch," Scarlet shouted after Lillian as she stormed away.

Lillian didn't look back as she headed to the bar and ordered four shots of tequila which she downed one after the other.

"Lillian…" Nick said into her ear, his hand coming to wrap around her waist.

"What?" she asked, downing yet another shot of tequila.

"That's enough," Nick said. "I'm taking you home." He picked up her purse and phone from the bar and quickly punched in a message to Ruby telling her that he was taking Lillian home and not to worry.

He then went outside and signalled a taxi, his arms never once leaving her waist. They quietly entered the taxi and as soon as they were sitting down, seatbelts fastened and Nick had told the taxi driver the address, Lillian curled up into his side and sobbed. Nick ran his hand through her hair whilst his other hand held hers tightly in her lap.

When they arrived at her flat, Nick helped her out of the taxi and up to the front door. He unlocked the door and she bolted past him for the bathroom. She hugged the toilet seat as the little of her dinner that she had eaten and the several shots of tequila made their way back out of her system.

Nick came in and handed her a glass of water and crouched beside her, brushing her white hair out of the way and rubbed circles on her back.

"It's okay, Lils. We can talk when you want to, but just so you know. I'm here for you," he said as he continued to rub circles on her back.

She sat up, her eyes red and puffy and her insides aching.

"I'm sorry," she said, accepting his hand as they both stood up and walked through to her bedroom. He found her some clothes to change into and helped her out of her shoes and dress and into a baggy shirt and a pair of baggy shorts. He helped her into bed and curled up beside her.

"Hey, Lils. What's going on?" Nick asked, placing a soft kiss to her temple.

Lillian sighed and cuddled into Nick.

"I was jealous…" she responded, hiding her face from him.

He bent down and gently cradled her face in his hands, making her look up at him. "There was nothing to be jealous of," he said, kissing her forehead again.

"I heard them in the toilets. Scarlet said she didn't think I deserved to be with you and she was going to take you away from me…" Lillian said between sobs.

Nick wiped the tears from her eyes. "Lillian, to me, no one will ever be as beautiful, funny and charming as you. She could have thrown herself at me naked and I still wouldn't have noticed. Yeah, we danced but as soon as I saw you coming towards me, all I wanted was to have you in my arms again."

Lillian hiccupped as she tried to stop sobbing. "Really?"

"Really," Nick said, scattering kisses over her face, shoulders, arms and hands.

Lillian giggled, feeling happy for the first time since they had started dinner.

"Feeling better?" Nick asked as he rolled Lillian to lie underneath him.

She nodded her head, smiling brightly at him, her eyes sparkling with happiness.

"Will we continue what we started earlier?" he said, laying a kiss on his initials behind her ear.

"Mmm," was Lillian's reply as she manoeuvred Nick onto his back and rolled them over, giggling the entire time.

Chapter Eight

The sky was setting, leaving a beautiful pinky-orange hue in its wake. Nick and Lillian walked across the cold, hard ground, watching the snow fall lightly around them. Lillian shuddered, wrapping her arms around her to keep some of the warmth in. She was frozen to the bone but enjoying herself far too much to call it a night.

Nick came up behind her and wrapped a blanket around her shoulders as they strolled through the market with coloured lights all around them. There were stalls of every shape and size and an ice rink in the centre of everything.

Lillian giggled and grabbed hold of Nick's hand, the excitement visible in her eyes. She pulled him along as she dashed between the stalls looking at all the pretty lights and exciting things being sold.

"I have something extra special to show you," Nick whispered into Lillian's ear. She beamed at him as he took her by the hand and dragged her away from the hustle and bustle. They walked through a set of gardens with twinkling lights, the moon shining over them, illuminating everything in its path.

They walked, Nick leading the way, until they reached a bend in the road. They followed the bend and Lillian stopped suddenly, her eyes going wide.

Nick wrapped his arms around her and whispered in her ear, "Beautiful, isn't it?"

Before them stood a water fountain, colourful magic swirling around it, playfully shooting streams of water into the air. The magic danced around the fountain, intertwining with the water reaching out to them. Lillian slowly stepped forward, reaching out to the magic. As soon as her hand touched the beautiful red magic in front of her, she felt the warmth wrap around her and push Nick over to her, enveloping them both in love and passion, making all her feelings feel heightened.

She wrapped her arms around his neck and started toying with the strands of hair at the base of his neck. His lips met hers, and he gently kissed her. His gentleness turned to urgency as his lips worshipped hers. It was more than Lillian could have ever hoped for. She revelled in his closeness and the passion he showed her with that kiss.

As they pulled apart, Nick wrapped his hand around hers and pulled her into the fountain. Lillian squealed as she closed her eyes, bracing herself for the impact of the cold water but it never came.

Slowly, she opened her eyes and inhaled deeply at the sight before her.

"Welcome to the hidden side of Edinburgh. This is the magical village. There's a little cafe that I want to show you and a bookstore that you will absolutely adore."

Lillian's eyes opened wide and she jumped up and down in excitement. She had never seen anything as magnificent as the sight before her,

He offered her his elbow and she smiled as she hooked her arm through his and followed him, absolutely amazed at everything going on around them. The magic was buzzing in the air, everything felt electric. Every shop was colourful, filled with bright lights and she didn't know where to look first. Nick opened a door in front of them and ushered her in. They walked up to the counter and Lillian started to eye up everything delicious that was available.

"Everything has a special addition to it. These ones have a dash of courage, these have a pinch of lust, these have a smidge of calmness. It's like your hot drinks can get a shot of syrup in them to help with feelings. When I first came here, I thought it was a brilliant idea." Nick explained.

"Hmm, I like the look of this one," she said pointing at a cupcake with creamy red frosting and multicoloured sprinkles on top.

He looked at the tag, filled with a hint of lust and admiration.

The smile that spread across her face made Nick realise that he was probably going to sincerely regret bringing her here, but for now he would be a good sport and play along with her little game.

Nick ordered and paid for the cakes and drinks as Lillian went to get a seat. She chose a booth by the window and as Nick approached, she sat admiring the night sky.

As he got closer Lillian smiled and took the tray from him so he could climb into the booth beside her. The seats were like something out an old 50s diner with a jukebox at the end of each table that you could request songs on.

He took the drinks off the tray and handed them to Lillian before doing the same with the baked goods.

Lillian inhaled the scent of the drink Infront of her, a creamy hot chocolate with peppermint syrup, topped with whipped cream, marshmallows and some chocolate flakes on top. She licked her lips and flashed Nick a dazzling smile before taking a long sip.

She put her cup down and Nick caught her eye, she watched as the tip of his pink tongue darted out and licked the whipped cream away from his upper lip. She sat mesmerised watching him. He noticed her watching and arched an eyebrow, pushing the plate towards her.

She cut the cake into smaller sections before taking a bite and moaning at how delicious it tasted. So smooth and chocolatey, rich and decadent. Heaven on a plate.

"This maybe wasn't such a good idea," Nick said, staring intently at her, the majority of his drink already finished. She looked up and the colour started to rise in her cheeks from the intensity of the look Nick was giving her. His pupils were fully dilated, and he kept running his hands through his hair, giving it a dishevelled look, the black strands falling to frame his face.

"Are you okay?" Lillian asked, reaching out and grabbing his hand, forgetting about the food that was left on the table.

Nick smiled at her, flushing lightly, a cheeky look appearing on his face.

"I think these drinks and cakes may have worked a little too well," he said standing up and taking Lillian's hand, pulling her to her feet. "Do you mind if we leave before I can't control myself any longer? Who knows what I'll do." He cheekily smirked at her.

Lillian nodded, threw a couple of coins down onto the table and then led Nick out of the little cafe.

When they were out onto the street, Nick pulled Lillian into a quiet alley and pinned her against the wall. He skimmed his lips along her jaw, nibbling slightly as he went.

The next thing she knew, Lillian felt his hand at the back of her neck guiding her towards him and tilting her head, driving his lips into hers for a searing kiss. She returned the kiss with just as much force and passion, the food they had just eaten affecting her just as much as him.

His breath hitched and he slid his hand into her wild hair. She rose on her tiptoes and met his kiss halfway, tilting her head so his nose rested against her cheek.

His mouth was gentle at first, coaxing her lips as her blood bubbled through her veins. The tenderness made her head spin and she clutched at his coat for support. A growl rumbled through his chest and he pulled her closer roughly.

"Why can't I control myself around you?" he whispered into her neck.

"Who said I wanted you to?" Lillian responded, winking at him.

He growled, a low and animalistic sound and pulled her body flush against his.

She 'mmmed' in response and he smirked against her skin as she ran her hands up into his hair, that was still curly from his shower before they went out for the day.

Lillian shivered in Nick's arms, not sure if it was from the cold or the feeling of being in his arms.

"Let's get you home," he said, taking his leather jacket off and wrapped it around her shoulders. "I can think of the perfect way to warm you up." He nipped her earlobe gently with his teeth, wrapping her up in his embrace.

She nodded her head and leaned into him, sighing contently.

Lillian smiled as she looked at Nick. "Thank you for tonight. I have had a wonderful time," she said, taking his hand as they emerged from the fountain.

She felt the magic splash on her skin and smiled.

"It's my pleasure," Nick said, wrapping his arms around her waist yet again. He felt the need to be close to her, make her realise how much he needed her. She reached up to him, pulling him down to meet her lips.

He deepened the kiss almost instantly, teasing her mouth open and chasing her tongue with his, the effect of the cake still in his system. His body shifted and his hand skimmed, warm and sure, over her neck and into her hair. Lillian groaned softly and braced herself against his shoulders, amazed that kissing him always felt this intense. He tasted like cinnamon and chocolate.

As they separated, he ran his hands down from her hair to her waist, lightly tickling her as he went. She laughed silently and felt his mouth curve into a smile. Finally, she looked up, and his eyes were sparkling mischievously.

"What?" she asked, smiling brightly up at him.

He ran his hand through his hair as he threaded his fingers through hers with the other.

"Nothing. Just thinking about how happy I am," he replied, moving their intwined hands to his mouth and placing a gentle kiss there.

They walked in comfortable silence through the market before heading home, where they both fell into bed, not getting to sleep until the early hours of the morning.

Chapter Nine

Lillian knocked on the door and took a deep breath. She knew she could do this but she needed to hype herself up a little bit first. She heard footsteps approaching and the door opened emitting a warm glow.

"Ah, Lillian. A pleasure," the smiling face of Julius spoke as he stepped aside to let her in.

"I'm very sorry to just appear like this, but I wanted to come and apologise for the way that I acted the last time we were together. I hadn't expected anyone to mention my mother and it just brought on so many emotions that I hadn't been prepared to deal with," she explained as she stood in his hallway.

"Oh, child, enough. It's in the past. Is there anything else that I can help you with today?" he asked, letting her walk into his study.

"Well, if you have time, I would love to look some more into *Necromancy*, but only if you have the time. I don't want to impose," she said, playing with the hem of her coat.

"Of course, my dear. Have a seat. I'll go make tea and we can have a little look into it," he said, patting her shoulder gently.

She smiled at the man as he walked away and sat down over at the window again. As she sat down, she looked out over the grounds. It was spectacular. As she was admiring the view, a little robin appeared on the window ledge and started to peck the window. She gently opened the window, trying to avoid scaring the little bird away, but it stayed exactly where it was. She placed her hand out and the little bird hopped forward and nuzzled her fingers gently.

After a few minutes, Julius appeared back with two steaming cups of tea. "My dear," he said, handing her a cup. "Who is your little friend?"

"I'm not sure. She was on the window ledge and hasn't left yet," Lillian replied, as the little bird fluttered up and over to Julius, gently pecking him on the cheek before flying out the window. After the robin left, Lillian closed the window as Julius watched on in wonder.

"How peculiar," he muttered to himself, watching the wings fly out of sight.

She inhaled the deep scent and enjoyed the warmth hitting her face.

"Thank you," she said, cradling the cup to her chest.

Julius sat down at his desk, taking a deep sip of his drink.

"So *Necromancy*. Do you know much?" he asked, watching her intently.

Lillian smiled tentatively and responded, "Just that it's the supposed practice of communicating with the dead, especially in order to predict the future."

Julius smiled and happily clapped his hands. "What a great place to start!" he stated excitedly. "Have I ever told you about my friend, Rodney?"

Lillian smiled and nodded her head. "Yes, you told me about him and his wife, the Newar woman."

Julius nodded his head. "Ah yes. She was a very talented woman and she specialised in *Necromancy*. Where I learnt a lot of my stuff from," he said looking off to the corner of the room.

Lillian sat sipping her tea as she waited for Julius to come out of his daydream. He jumped with a start. "Sorry, my dear. I was a million miles away. Anyway." He took a deep sip of his tea. "*Necromancy* is the practice of magic or black magic involving communication with the dead — either by summoning their spirits as apparitions, visions or raising them bodily — for the purpose of divination, imparting the means to foretell future events, discover hidden knowledge, to bring someone back from the dead, or to use the dead as a weapon. Sometimes referred to as 'Death Magic', the term may also sometimes be used in a more general sense to refer to black magic or witchcraft."

He took another sip of his tea. "The word *necromancy* is adapted from late Latin *necromantia*, itself borrowed from post-classical Greek *ekromanteía*, a compound of ancient Greek *nekrós* meaning dead body and *manteía* meaning divination. This compound form was first used by Origen of Alexandria in the third century AD. The classical Greek term was *nekyia*, from the episode of the odyssey in which Odysseus visits the realm of the dead souls. I thought you would enjoy that fact as Nick said you liked literature."

He smiled as he watched her blush.

"You care for the boy," he said, changing the subject quickly.

Lillian, surprised by the change of subject, nodded her head. "Immensely," she stated matter-of-factly.

"Good. He needs you. He may never admit it, but he always will." He tipped the cup, drinking every last drop of his tea as Lillian did the same.

"Anyway, back to *Necromancy*. I take it you want to learn more about modern-day *Necromancy*. In the present day, *Necromancy* is more generally used as a term to describe manipulation of death and the dead, or the pretence thereof, like you said, and is often facilitated through the use of ritual magic or some other kind of occult ceremony. Contemporary séances, channelling and spiritualism verge on *Necromancy* when supposedly invoked spirits are asked to reveal future events or secret information. *Necromancy* may also be presented as *sciomancy*, a branch of theurgic magic."

Lillian nodded, taking mental notes as Julius spoke. "So if I ever wanted to practice this type of magic then I would need to do a ritual of some sort?" she asked.

Julius nodded his head. "Yes, but I recommend not doing this by yourself. Find someone else who practices this sort of magic or let me point you in the right direction. You are very powerful but I don't want you getting hurt," he said seriously.

She nodded her head, her brain whirring with information.

"Do you have any more books I could read please?" she asked. "I still have so many questions but only so much brain space to deal with this."

He nodded his head in understanding. "Of course, my dear, just give me a minute to find them." He started to walk out of the room and then stopped. "What am I thinking?"

He walked into the centre of the room and closed his eyes, he lifted his hands up over his head, magic danced around him, different shades of blue swirling around him, leaving his body and floating through the air. Lillian watched in awe as a book floated down from one of the shelves. She held out her arms as it fell into them and smiled as she felt the tingles of magic make their way up her arms and into her soul.

Julius smiled as he saw Lillian in her element.

She looked down at the book in her hands and read the title, "*Necromancy: The Rituals*, thank you so much."

Lillian skipped to the door and waved to Julius as she vanished from sight.

When she got home, she curled up on the bed and started reading, waiting for Nick to get home from seeing his friends.

"*Necromancers* needed to get into the right frame of mind. They'd wear the dead person's clothes and eat food that represented decay, like black bread. Once they'd slipped into a magical mood, they'd cast a circle and begin a conjuration. They'd burn hemlock, mandrake and opium to help get the atmosphere right.

"Some sources even claimed *necromancers* might mutilate or eat corpses though that's unlikely in the medieval period. These magicians used spells and incantations with a linguistic structure similar to those used in exorcisms. They took these rituals very seriously.

"But medieval *necromancers* believed only God's assistance could affect a physical resurrection. Instead, they conjured spirits. For Herbert Stanley Redgrove, ceremonial magic in the medieval period fell into three categories: 'White magic, Black magic, and *Necromancy*'. Redgrove draws a distinction between black magic, 'concerned with the evocation of demons and devils', and *Necromancy*, which was 'concerned with the evocation of the spirits of the dead'.

"Some *Necromancy* rituals require a 'sacrifice' but that doesn't always refer to killing a person. Offering hair or blood stood in for a sacrifice, though they often used animal blood in the process. Many *necromancers* chose 'sympathetic magic' when making requests of spirits. As an example, knocking two rocks together demonstrated the feud they wanted the spirits to start between two families."

"Following the Enlightenment, the practice seems to have moved into other areas, such as seances and spiritualism. Both involve asking spirits questions, prompting notions of *Necromancy* when querents ask about the future. The nineteenth-century introduction of cremation in the western world makes resurrecting the body impossible. It's hardly surprising that spiritualism offered a cleaner alternative with fewer (or no) religious overtones.

"And it's less messy to use a Ouija board to ask your dead uncle where he left a winning lottery ticket than making blood drinks. Largely, the cult of mourning begun during Queen Victoria's reign changed the way we think about death. Few would want to disturb the eternal rest of a loved one, and physically opening a grave remains the preserve of forensic specialists."

"Lillian, where are you?" Nick shouted through the house.

"Upstairs," she replied, flicking through the pages of the book.

He slowly toed open the door and smirked. "Why am I not surprised? Nose in a book," he said, jumping on the bed next to her.

She giggled as he launched himself at her, peppering kisses across her face.

"How drunk are you?" she asked as his fingers skimmed up her sides.

Nick placed his finger on his chin, mimicking being thoughtful. "I'm drunk enough to know that I have no inhibitions, but sober enough so you don't have to feel like you're taking advantage," he said, wiggling his eyebrows at her.

She laughed as he rolled on top of her, covering her mouth with his, the book completely forgotten about as it hit the floor with a thud.

A few hours later, Lillian was curled up into Nick's side, the book laid open between them. "Why *Necromancy*?" he asked as he turned the page.

Lillian sat up slightly, gathering the covers around her chest. "It may sound silly, but I want to see if there is a way to contact my mum. I have the chance to try so I really want to... It's silly, I know," she responded, closing the book and running her hands over the leather-bound cover.

"Hey, look at me," he said, tilting her head up so that their eyes met. "It is not silly. She is an important part of your life and always will be. If it helps you get closure, of course it's something to look into. Never doubt your abilities and trust your gut. If you feel like this is something you have to do, then do it." He bent down and kissed her gently.

As they broke apart, he looked at the time. "Okay, sleep. You have work tonight," he said, kissing the crown of her head before settling down beside her, tucking the covers around them.

"Thank you, Nick," she murmured before falling asleep.

Nick left the room to go and get some food. After about twenty minutes, he slid the door open and smiled as he entered. Lillian was bundled up in the covers, her book propped open in her hands, gently snoring away. He walked over to the bed and laid down beside her, placing a soft kiss on her forehead as he took the book from her hands. He turned and set the alarm for Lillian waking up for her shift that evening. He opened the book and decided to start reading the page Lillian had left off at, content at just being beside her.

Chapter Ten

Lillian sat at the table on her break and logged into her social media accounts. The joys of working this ridiculous time of night were that none of her friends were awake so she usually just scrolled through the different socials to kill time.

She logged into one and the first thing she was greeted with was a picture of her and Nick messing about in the snow on their date the other night. She smiled at the memory of his arms wrapped around her, keeping her warm against the cold.

The picture had been up for a few hours and already had thousands of comments. She smiled to herself as she clicked on them. Some would be from the people who they streamed with or spoke with on a regular basis.

Don't understand why he would want her? Look at the state of it.

What does he see in her? He could do so much better.

Look at the size of her? Doesn't she look in a mirror, like ever?

Lillian sat staring at the comments, the majority following the same pattern and felt sick. She stood up quickly and made her way to the bathroom, tears leaking from the corner of her eyes. They were jealous, that was all. She knew this deep inside but it still didn't stop the aching pain in her chest.

She collapsed to the ground of the bathroom and sobbed.

When she eventually made it out of the toilet cubicle, eyes red and puffy, she spoke quietly to her manager saying she needed to go home and wouldn't be in for the rest of the week and apologised before fleeing out the door.

She made it home in record time, throwing herself on the bed, tears flowing freely now, and curled up into a ball. She had never been a particularly positive person about her looks. When she was younger, she was picked on for everything, from her hair to her curvy size. She wasn't overly big, had curves in the right places but had a little bit of belly that she had never been happy with. Only recently had she felt confident to wear certain types of clothes and now everything she had been trying to achieve since she was thirteen, all her self-love and self-appreciation had gone out of the window with a few lousy comments.

She fell asleep on the bed, hugging herself and crying into her pillow. She hadn't felt so low in a long time.

The sun was blasting through the cracks in the curtains when Lillian was awoken by knocking at the door. She reached for her phone to check the time, seven a.m. and noticed twenty-five missed calls from Nick. She grabbed her laptop and opened the page of the social media yet again, ignoring the constant banging on the front door. She got lost in the negativity of the picture, all good memories from that night, now being replaced with negative ones that she couldn't shake. She didn't need to know she was fat, or had stupid coloured hair or that it was frizzy or that she would squash Nick in bed. Every single comment crushed her inside. She could feel her magic thrum around her, as her feelings got the better of her.

She let out another sob, unable to control it any more. As she rubbed her eyes with the back of her hands, she felt the magic shift in the house around her and she knew Nick had given up waiting and let himself in.

"That was some pretty powerful magic Lil. You'd think you didn't want to see me or something," he said as he swung her bedroom door open.

He took one look at her and quickly kicked his shoes off and joined her on the bed, gathering her up in his arms. "*Ssh*," he said, comforting her, running one hand through her hair and rubbing circles on her back with the other. "Whatever it is. It will be okay."

He wiped a tear from her cheek and laid a gentle kiss on her cheek as she sobbed.

"Why… why… Why would you want me?"

Nick stopped his movements and looked at her.

"Hey, what do you mean, why would I want you?" he asked, pulling her into his embrace tighter.

"They were right. Every single one of them. Why would you want me? They are so beautiful and witty and everything I'll never be…" She cried hard at this. It was unattractive tears, but she had lost control hours ago and couldn't stop now.

"If you are talking about the comments, then there is only one thing I agree with. That you should look in a mirror," he said cuddling her tighter.

"What do you mean?" She cried harder. Did he really agree with them? "If you don't want me and are scared to break this bond, just do it now. I'm already hurting. Just rip the Band-Aid off." Every single word she stated was punctuated with a sob.

Nick took her face in both of his hands. "I didn't mean it like that at all. What I meant was that you don't see yourself clearly. You are beautiful." He kissed her cheek. "Smart." He kissed her cheek again. "Sexy as hell." He kissed her softly on the lips. "And most importantly. All. Mine!"

Lillian sat up and turned to face him, kissing him soundly on the lips. She threw her leg over his and straddled his lap as she continued to kiss him, turning all the hurt and pain she'd felt for the past ten hours into the passion and admiration she felt for the man in front of her.

She wove her hands up into his hair and tugged slightly eliciting a low moan from him as she continued to kiss him senseless.

She pulled away from him, moving her lips to his neck, placing kisses as she went.

"Lillian, you have no idea how much I want to continue this," she gently nibbled on his earlobe and he groaned. "But we need to talk. You are upset and I don't want that to be the reason you are doing this. I don't want this to be something you regret, especially due to the circumstances surrounding it."

Lillian leaned forward again, kissing his lips tenderly. "You are far too good to me," she whispered, placing her head on his shoulder as he wrapped his arms tightly around her waist.

"You are amazing Lillian. Ignore those comments. It doesn't matter what they think about you. All that matters is what you think about you and I want you to know how absolutely crazy I am about you too."

She threw herself down on the bed beside him and he wrapped his arms around her.

"Come meet my parents?" he quietly whispered, "I want you to know that there is no doubt in my mind about you."

She slowly nodded her head before her eyes fluttered shut and she fell into a peaceful sleep. As she drifted off into unconsciousness, the last thought that flitted through her head was how much she loved this man.

Chapter Eleven

Nick grabbed Lillian's hand. "You're shaking," he whispered in her ear.

"I'm just a little nervous. It's a big deal meeting your parents," she replied. He shook his head and laughed.

"You'll be absolutely fine. You are amazing, I'm sure they'll see that as soon as they meet you."

She ran her hand over her dress to get out any creases in it and let out a sigh.

"You have this. You can do this," she muttered to herself.

They walked up along driveway and Lillian let out a loud gasp as the house appeared before her.

"Your parents live here?" she asked, looking up at the tall granite building in front of her. It was massive and very intimidating. The snow lay thick on the ground underfoot. The icy wind whipped through her hair, chilling her to the bone. The late afternoon sun was setting, casting a red glow across the sparkling landscape. A sigh escaped her lips as they approached a wrought iron gate. Barren trees cascaded high above them, creating eerie shadows.

The walk from the gate was long and slow. As the feeling of anticipation bubbled up inside of her, only one thing kept her nerves calm. The feeling of Nick's hand interlocked with hers.

The walk to the Victorian looking mansion was over much too soon and before they knew it, they were standing at the entrance. The door loomed above them, large and heavy, carved with different astrological signs. She sighed once again. Nick reached over and placed a small kiss on her cheek.

"It'll be okay," he whispered into her ear. She smoothed down her dress once more as Nick knocked on the door.

A little old woman, with grey curls piled on top of her head and laugh lines surrounding her eyes answered the door and smiled as she saw Nick.

"Mrs Miller, a pleasure as always," Nick said bowing slightly.

"Always so formal Nicholas," she replied. "And who is this lovely lady?"

"This is Lillian," he said, placing his hand gently on her back. Lillian held out her hand and Mrs Miller took it, shaking gently.

"It's a pleasure Mrs Miller," she said smiling at the old lady. She had a friendly expression and made Lillian feel at ease which she was very grateful for.

"Your mother and father are waiting for you in the sun lounge. I'll take your coats, you know the way," she said, winking at Nick.

Lillian took a deep breath and put her happiest face on. They approached a door and he rubbed a circle on her lower back, letting her know they were about to approach the room his mother and father were in.

He opened the door and smiled at his parents.

"Mother, father," he said. He walked over to a woman with black hair, pinned up in an elegant chignon. She wore a knee-length black dress and dark tights. She was beautiful in every sense of the word and you could feel the magic emanating off her. His father placed the book he had been reading down on the table and as he looked up a smirk that was identical to Nick's. He looked exactly like his son, just older. His black hair was tinted with different shades of grey and he wore black slacks and a black shirt and jumper.

"Mother, father. This is Lillian Robertson, the girl I am absolutely crazy about," he said, walking back over to her and pulling out a chair for her to sit on.

She smiled up at him as she took a seat. "It's a pleasure to meet you, Mr and Mrs Madden."

"She's polite, I like her," his father said, his voice cool and flat. He reached over and picked his book back up.

She looked down at her hands and entwined them on her lap.

"So, Miss Robertson. What do you plan on gaining from your relationship with my son?" his mother asked, her cold eyes staring straight into Lillian's soul. Lillian swallowed and looked down at the table.

"Mother, that is inappropriate," Nick stated, grabbing one of Lillian's hands.

"I'm just asking," she said, pouring a cup of tea out for them all. "What are your intentions?"

"I intend to see how this goes. We are very compatible and I am enjoying spending time with him and getting to know him. I have no intentions apart from pure ones," Lillian said, trying to keep her voice steady.

Nick squeezed her hand and smiled at her. "Mother, this is not an intervention. We came here for you to get to know her and not give her the fifth-degree. You can either accept this or we will leave… Which would you prefer?"

Nick's father sighed and put his book back down. "She doesn't mean anything. We already know a lot about Miss Robertson."

"Please, call me Lillian," she said quietly.

"If you wish," his father said. "Well, we know quite a bit about her. She's been on our radar since long before you two got together."

Nick looked at his father and furrowed his eyebrows. The moment he realised where his father was going with his story, he stood up throwing his seat back. "No! It can't be. How can this be happening? She's not even fully magical."

His father and mother both looked at him disapprovingly. "We raised you better than that Nicholas," his mother scolded.

"Oh, to hell with my upbringing. I care about this girl. You can't be doing this…" Nick said, anger evident in his tone.

"Can someone tell me what's going on?" Lillian asked, looking around at everyone in the room.

"My dear, how much magical knowledge do you have?" his father asked, looking over at Lillian.

"Not a huge amount, but I've been reading up on stuff," she explained. "Nick's given me books to do some research. My mother died when I was young and my father lost all motivation towards magic after that." Nick reached across and wiped a stray tear from her cheek.

"I'm so sorry you had to go through that my dear. Losing a family member is never ideal. Well, I take it Nick hasn't explained much about our family?"

She shook her head.

"Father," Nick warned.

"She deserves to know Nicholas."

"No!" Nick shouted slamming his fist on the table. "She's my soulmate! Don't you dare ruin this for me! I don't care if it's selfish!" He lifted his sleeve to show her initials on his wrist.

"Nicholas, it's destiny. She deserves to know the whole truth. It's not just about her. It's about her family too. Do not deprive her of this," his father warned.

The entire time this conversation was happening, Nick's mother was observing Lillian.

"Nicholas, my dear. I would like a word with Lillian. We shall walk in the gardens," she said, noticing his glare. "Don't look at me like that. I shall be civil."

Nick's mother held out her elbow, indicating that Lillian should link her arm through it. She did as was expected and the two of them walked through some glass double doors into the most glorious gardens Lillian had ever seen.

"This is beautiful," she said to his mother, admiring the view around her. There were flowers everywhere, beautiful multicoloured roses, lilies of every shade, sunflowers all admiring the sun.

"Lillian, I need to apologise. I'm very protective over my son, as any mother would be, but our family tree is basically the reason why I am so worried about him. Females often try to get into our family and I have to protect what's ours."

"Mrs Madden," Lillian started.

"Please call me Victoria," his mother said.

"Victoria, I don't need an apology. I understand completely. I may not have told him yet, but I love your son with all my heart and would never do anything to hurt him," Lillian said in the most sincere voice she had ever used.

"I know. I can tell by the way you two look at each other. You need to know more about us though. I will tell you about my side of the family and I will leave my husband to tell you about his. You said you were doing research. Have you come across the head of the magical world?"

Lillian thought hard for a minute. "There is a king and queen that rules over everyone and makes sure that every rule is followed? No illegal magic or harming of non-magical people."

Victoria smiled. "That's correct. However, they are not the king and queen to our family. To me, they would be Mother and Father."

"You… You're a princess?" Lillian asked, shocked.

Victoria nodded her head.

"I am so sorry, your majesty. If I had known, I would have addressed you with the correct title," Lillian apologised.

"Hush child," Victoria said, stopping, placing a blanket Lillian hadn't seen her carrying and taking a seat on one of the benches surrounded by rose bushes. "None of that. You can understand now why I was the way I was when you first came in. I worry that if someone is interested in my son, it is for status purposes or money. Seeing how passionately he stood up for you and how you defended yourself here to me, I realise that it is so much more than that. Can I see your mark?" she asked.

Lillian smiled and moved the hair from behind her ear... "I didn't even notice it to start with," Lillian said. "It was Nick who saw it first."

"Hmmm." Victoria waved her hand in front of them, a rose appearing in front of Lillian's face. "I suppose we should head back inside and make sure that they haven't killed each other. I know what their tempers are like." She laughed as if remembering something.

They walked through the gardens making small conversation. Lillian held the door open for Victoria.

"Gentlemen," she said as she glided into the room. "Glad to see no blood has been shed."

Nick snorted, "As if I would get blood on the furniture, you'd have me gutted alive."

Victoria laughed. "Come in dear," she said to Lillian, pulling out a chair for her. "Tea?"

Lillian nodded, gently taking the cup from Nick. "Thank you."

"So, my dear, you now understand Victoria's side of the family, so now is my turn to tell you mine and how you come into this whole story."

Lillian took a sip of her tea as she waited for him to continue. Nick took a seat next to her and laid his free hand on her thigh.

"Okay, so I knew your mother." Lillian's eyes went as wide as saucers and she felt Nick's hand tighten on her thigh in support.

"Your mother was not magical, per se, but she did work within the magical community. She worked for me. I gave her powers to use that any non-magical person would be able to. I suppose, the best way to describe the job I do, would be to compare myself to an undertaker maybe. Although rather than just helping bury people, I take them on to the next life."

"So you're essentially, death personified?" Lillian asked, "How did my mother help with this if you don't mind me asking?"

"Not at all, my dear. Your mother brought them to me. She was given a locating spell. It would tell her the time and location where the people were and she would take them to the office."

Lillian swallowed. "Alive?"

Nick's father looked at her and raised his eyebrow. "That's what the magic was for. So she would never have to physically take someone's life. She would give them a potion or cast a spell and then that was the hard part done. They sometimes fight back and unfortunately one of the times your mother was out on the job, she didn't have enough potions and magic with her. The warlock was too powerful. I'm sorry my dear."

Nick grabbed her hand and squeezed tightly.

"I understand that this is a lot of information to take in and there is a little bit more, but that can wait for another time."

Lillian looked at Nick's father. "Please just tell me now?" she pleaded. It felt like her heart was breaking. The woman she had grown up admiring, was tainted and she felt like she was slowly drowning.

"You're the next in line to take this position over. It's in your family's bloodline. We weren't due to have this conversation until your 25th birthday, but dear Nicholas here, helped speed up our meeting."

"Wait, what?" Lillian said, looking over at Nick. The fire burned in her eyes and Nick instantly paled.

"Lils, I swear, I didn't know any of that. I just wanted them to meet you," he said, the tone of anguish in his voice. "I was trying to show you how much you mean to me and how important you are to me. I didn't know any of this." He took a hold of her hand and rubbed his thumb over her knuckles gently.

"Doesn't matter," Lillian said, her voice staying calm but removing her hand from his grasp.

"My dear, would you like to go for a walk to discuss this?" his father asked. "Out into the garden for some fresh air, or I can give you a tour of the house as we talk?"

Lillian thought for a few seconds. "A tour sounds lovely, Mr Madden."

"Please, call me Steve," he said, holding out his arm.

They left the room with Nick pleading for Lillian to listen to him. She ignored him and walked out the room. As soon as they left the room, there was a loud clatter on the other side of the door as he roared with anger. She let out a soft sigh. They had never fought before.

"Don't hold it against him my dear. He didn't know. He tries to spend as little time with the side of things as possible. I'm glad he has you."

Lillian sighed. "So this job? Is it a full-time thing? Is there a book on it?"

Steve laughed. "He was right about you. Follow me this way. I shall take you to the library and we shall forego the rest of the tour. You are always welcome to take some books home with you. Nick will be joining you. Your special bond will make it safer for you both. After the tragedy with your mother, I don't want anything to happen to you."

He opened the door and Lillian stood in the doorway in awe.

"This is incredible," she exclaimed. Walls upon walls of books spread their way around the room. A large window adorned the furthest wall looking out onto the gardens and a large lake. The sun had now set and there was a slight glitter on the snow that covered the landscape.

As she was admiring the room, Steve walked to one of the shelves and grabbed several books for her, placing them on the elegantly carved table in the middle of the room.

"For you my dear," he said, taking a seat in front of the fire and summoning a glass of whisky. "Would you like a drink?"

Lillian shook her head, already having started reading the books laid out for her. Steve smirked. He knew she would make a great addition to his team; she was studious, enthusiastic and from what he saw, had a fireball of an attitude. He just needed to see what her magical ability was like.

Lillian noticed Steve observing her, but kept her head down reading. She wanted to gain as much information as possible while she had access to so many books. After about twenty minutes, he excused himself to go check on his wife and son. She grabbed the books and walked over to the window to take a seat there.

Lillian left the library with the books under her arms. Mrs Miller was out in the hallway when she got to the front door.

"Hi dear, are you okay?" she asked as Lillian approached.

"Yes, thank you. Can I please have my coat?" Lillian asked politely.

Mrs Miller nodded. "Nick is waiting for you outside. He said I was to let you know when you came down the stairs."

"Thank you very much. It was lovely to meet you. Can you say goodbye to Mr and Mrs Madden for me?" she said, putting her coat around her shoulders and buttoning it up.

She left, waving at Mrs Miller, as she shut the door, she saw Nick sitting underneath a large tree with his jacket pulled tight around him.

When he saw her, he got up and sprinted over to her side. "Lillian…"

"You never thought it would be a good idea to mention any of this to me? The fact that you lied when you said that you didn't really practice magic, that your mother is a princess in the world of magic, something I know very little about, thereby making you a prince. But the worst part is that you also didn't think to tell me that your father is essentially the Grim fucking Reaper!" she shouted emphasising how upset she was by hitting his chest. She turned away from him, walking away quickly, her coat billowing behind her.

"Lillian, wait…" he started, but she quickly interrupted him.

"So how did you manage it then? How did you manage to set up the whole soulmate thing to make all this more convenient? Just wait to find someone willing, someone who actually cared and use them to get your father's plan into action?"

He raked a hand through his hair as she vented. "I promise you, all of that is real. I didn't pretend any of it. You are my other half, please just give me a chance to explain…"

She whirled around on the spot and raised an eyebrow. "I'll give you exactly five minutes. Go," she said looking down at her watch.

"Oh erm, well…"

"You have four and a half," she responded.

"Lillian," he said, taking a step towards her. He looked her straight in the eyes and gave her a small smile.

"No, don't you dare 'Lillian' me and give me that look, Nick. I was falling for you big time you egotistical jerk of a man. I don't even want to be near you right now!" She let out a scream of frustration.

The anger got the better of Nick. "Lillian, you listen to me right now. I didn't know that this was the case. The fact that you would accuse me of setting this up or using you. That hurts. You know me!" he shouted, kicking the ground in front of him, dust flying into the air.

Lillian growled, magic radiating off her. "I will see you later when we have work to do, apparently." She disappeared in a flash of red and dark green light.

"Fuck," he muttered to himself, heading back up to the house. He realised he had made a mistake by not telling her in advance but he thought she would give him a chance to explain. This chance never came. His bloody father had to ruin it. He ran his hand through his hair again. He couldn't blame his father. Not really. He should have told her, but he didn't want to scare her. The soulmate aspect was enough to terrify someone without adding to it his lineage. He knew he had to think and sort this out, but at this moment in time all he wanted was a large drink.

Chapter Twelve

Lillian appeared home in a fit of rage. She knew she shouldn't really be angry but couldn't help it. It was bubbling up inside of her, her magic sizzling along her skin. She aimed her frustration towards the fireplace and it burst into a fiery rage.

She sighed as she threw herself down onto her sofa and raked her hands through her hair, tugging slightly. She hadn't meant to accuse him of hiding stuff from her but she was struggling to control her emotions. Everything just felt too much for her. She looked out the large bay window at the wintery colours that filled her garden. It was at this moment that she knew what she needed to do to clear her head.

She walked to the front door and grabbed her coat and scarf, bundling herself up warm, before heading into the kitchen to make herself a cup of tea in her flask. As the kettle boiled, she tapped her foot impatiently.

She put the lid on her cup and headed out the back door, locking it behind her.

She walked up the length of the garden kicking snow with the toe of her boot, sending it flying into the air. She watched as the little flurries of white landed on top of her black boots.

She carried on up the length of the garden and toward the wrought iron gate at the back. She slowly opened it to avoid disturbing the spiders that had built their homes, the squeaking of the hinges the only thing to be heard above the wind.

She walked along the path stepping from stone to stone with heavy steps, her boots clattering against the ground.

She knew exactly where she was heading as she took a long sip of her tea. She pulled her scarf tighter around her and cursed herself for not bringing her gloves with her.

She rounded the corner, scattering a large pile of snow that had been cleared to the side of the path with her long strides when she saw the destination that she was heading for.

Her stride started to speed up to nearly a jog. She came to a sudden halt at another wrought iron gate which she flung open and took a total of ten steps before she threw herself at the ground, not caring about how cold the ground was or that she was sat in a pile of snow. Her arms wrapped around herself, and she openly began to sob.

"Mum…" She cried, touching the headstone in front of her. There were roses and sunflowers that were starting to wither away in front of the grave and Lillian realised how much she had been neglecting the site since she had met Nick. This brought on more tears and Lillian picked up the flowers and launched them into the air. As they floated down, they slowly began to revive and turned the vivid colours that they had been a few months earlier. They landed in a circle around Lillian and her mother's grave as Lillian looked around her.

"I miss you," she whispered as the wind whipped around her in a soothing hug. Lillian smiled as she felt her mother's essence in the hug and couldn't help but shiver. She took her cup and swallowed the contents of it.

"Mum, I've met someone. You would love him. He's polite, a true gentleman. He looks after me, even when I forget to myself. There is only one issue. He's the son of Mr Madden and I just found out everything. I'm meant to take over from you with his work." Lillian started as the wind whipped through her hair, making plaits in it as she spoke.

"I don't know what to do. I'm scared. I can't end up like you, I can't lose Nick either, Mum. I love him. I haven't told him this, but it's true. I can't think straight it's so true. I wish you were here Mum. I need you right now."

The wind whipped around her and she smiled despite all her mixed feelings.

"I know you're here, but I want a hug. The kind only a mother can give. I love you Mum."

The wind spun around her, and the flowers surrounding Lillian lifted from the floor once more to spell out 'I love you'.

Lillian smiled and patted the stone before standing up again. "Thanks Mum. I knew you would help."

She turned to walk away not noticing the figure hovering at the other side of the graveyard. The person who had seen the whole exchange. She didn't notice as she walked away that the figure came closer to her mother's grave, collected the flowers and then left in the opposite direction.

Lillian, oblivious to everything, headed home to think, to plan her new job and to try and work out how she was going to make this relationship with Nick work. But first, a nice warm bath.

Chapter Thirteen

It was three days before she was willing to even come close to the house. The beautiful house that belonged to the man who ordered death amongst warlocks and witches who had betrayed their oath and the queen Princess of the magical world. She had started on her task and was furious at the fact that she was having to do it on her own. He got her into this mess, he should have at least been there helping. If he cared, he would have been. The long flowing fabric of her coat billowed out behind her as she strode forward, determination powering her actions. She burst through the door with a flick of the wrist and sighed.

"Are you sober?" she asked, exasperated, trying not to look at him directly.

"I'm moderately functional," he replied.

"I'll take that as a no then." The humour in his voice pissed her off and she marched forward, grabbing the tumbler of amber liquid out of his hand and swallowing it, burning her throat on the way down.

"We have like five people we need to find right now and you're sitting here losing yourself in the bottom of a bloody bottle." She scrubbed a hand over her face.

"Actually, it's more like eight," he responded, looking her straight in the eye.

She threw the glass against the opposite wall, a growl escaping her throat. "Oh, sorry, I wasn't specific enough."

He looked up at her and smiled as he summoned another glass.

"All that blood looks good on you. It really brings out the colour of your eyes."

She rolled her eyes at him. "You're a psychopath."

"I prefer creative," he retorted, pouring more into his glass.

She shrugged her coat off and placed it over the back of one of the winged-back chairs. "Awfully confident, aren't you?"

He swirled the liquid around the glass in his hand, eyeing it before swallowing the whole lot.

"I can kill every person that we are looking for before they even get up off their sorry asses. Skills like that do wonders for a person's self-confidence."

"Will you just get up," she said, sighing, running a hand through her blood-soaked hair, trying to separate the strands that were now stuck together. "I want to get a shower before the debriefing. I'm sure your mother and father would love to see me like this," she said sarcastically, indicating her ripped clothing and exposed skin.

A growl escaped from deep in his throat and he stood up with such force that the chair toppled behind him. Her eyes narrowed, watching his lean frame approach.

"What are you doing?" she snarled, clenching her fists, stepping back until her back hit the wall.

He focused his eyes onto hers and simply whispered, "This."

He tilted her face up and slanted his lips against hers, biting violently at her bottom lip, grabbing her wrists and pinning them above her head to the wall. She was so shocked that she didn't respond in the way that she originally wanted to by kneeing him somewhere that it would hurt, but instead did what came naturally and moaned, melting into him and kissing him back just as vigorously.

He was surprised and smirked throughout the kiss. He groaned in appreciation, low and animalistic.

Her breath was heavy, her eyes glazed over when they eventually separated.

"Whatever possessed you to do that…"

"Mine." He breathed out. He took a step back and looked at her. She was flushed and breathing heavy, and he was so grateful that he could still produce that sort of reaction from her. He thought that he had lost her for good.

"I was going to say, before you interrupted me. Whatever possessed you to do that should possess you all of the time." She ran her hands down his chest. "You aren't forgiven you know," she said quietly, brushing a stray hair behind his ear.

The smirk that appeared on his face was breathtaking. "I know. I discovered something whilst we were apart."

"What's that?"

"I've discovered that I really do love you."

"And when did you realise this?" She arched an eyebrow at him and folded her arms over her chest.

"Since every decision I have made, good or bad, has revolved around you. From the moment you ended up on the floor of my studio, from the first moment you tuned into one of my videos."

She exhaled. "You can't blame me for the decisions that you make or for the secrets that you have kept."

"The first video I watched of yours, you were already in a relationship," she stated matter-of-factly, tapping her foot.

"Which ended two days later... I made a mistake," he muttered. "Everything happened so quickly when we met. I was scared and didn't want to risk losing the best thing that ever happened to me. I didn't want you to run away and risk losing my soulmate. You have no idea how much it hurts to be away from you." He reached out to grab hold of her hand. She let him and he exhaled not realising that he had been holding his breath.

"Why didn't you come find me?" she asked, looking at their interwoven fingers.

He shrugged slightly. "I didn't think you would want to be found." The hurt in his voice was evident and she could feel the pain that he was feeling.

Her gaze softened and she slowly lifted up onto her tiptoes and placed a soft kiss on the edge of his nose.

"Say it again," she whispered, looking up at him through her eyelashes.

He closed the distance between them again, placing a hand on each of her cheeks.

"Lillian Robertson, I love you with all of my heart and soul and everything in between." He bent down and kissed her sweetly.

"Oh Nick. I love you too, you egotistical, maniac of a man, but I am severely pissed off with you right now," she said playfully, swatting his chest. "Let's go back to yours so I can have a shower, you can sober up and we can have a conversation about this new job of ours?"

"Ours?" Nick asked, his eyebrows furrowing in confusion.

"Oh. So your father decided not to tell you that you've been roped into the family business too then? Great surprise!" she said sarcastically. "Your parents are lovely, but I don't think I quite trust them."

"That makes two of us, my love. That makes two of us. Unfortunately, I knew about the job, I just thought I had gotten away without being roped into it," he said, wrapping his arm around her, before whispering, 'Adventure achieved' and the two of them being whisked away in several flashes of colour.

Chapter Fourteen

The shower was exactly what she needed. She felt revived as she wrapped herself up in a large, fluffy towel and padded through to the bedroom that she now spent more time in than her own.

"Better?" Nick asked, lounging on the bed.

"Much," she replied rubbing a towel through her white curls. "How long do we have until we have to leave?"

"Mmmm, long enough for my amazing girlfriend to get her cute little butt over here and give me a kiss."

She sashayed over to him and threw herself into his lap, burrowing her face in the crook of his neck. She raked her fingers down his chest, slowly undoing each button of his shirt in the process. She peppered kisses on his skin, making sure to pay attention to the spot that caused him to let out a low guttural moan.

"My dear, as much as I would love to keep this going, we definitely don't have enough time to continue this and not piss off 'daddy dearest'."

Lillian let out a giggle and removed herself from his lap. As she left the room, she swayed her hips from side to side and dropped the towel in the process, sending a wink over her shoulder to Nick. He let out a groan and threw himself back onto the bed.

Lillian stood in front of the mirror and smiled. Never in her life had she felt this confident. Normally she would never stand looking at herself in the mirror with clothes on, never mind completely nude. She took in the blush that spread over her body and admired her curves. She felt sexy and proud of the way she looked.

Stepping away from the mirror she turned to look at the outfits in the wardrobe. She grabbed a skin-tight bodysuit and a pair of leather trousers and chucked on a pair of boots, she ruffled her hair up and applied a little eyeliner before heading out to see if Nick was ready.

When she walked into the bedroom, he was still laying on the bed, his shirt hanging open, staring at the ceiling.

"Ready?" she asked, trying her best to look all innocent, despite the fact that she looked like a supermodel.

Nick looked at her and let out a low wolf whistle. "Whatever I did to get you to be my soulmate, I will do a million times over. Holy shit, you are stunning," he said walking over to her and wrapping his arms around her waist.

"Ready to go?" she asked, placing a gentle kiss against his lips. He nodded as she thought of his parents' house and they vanished in a flash of colour.

She confidently took his hand and strode up the path to the house. She knocked on the door and smiled when Mrs Miller opened the door. "Lillian, Nick, how lovely to see you both," she said, moving to the side to let them in, "How are you both doing?"

"I'm good thank you," Lillian said. "Sorry to be abrupt, but Mr Madden is expecting us."

Mrs Miller smiled. "Of course dear. You both know where you are going?"

Nick nodded his head and he wrapped his arm around Lillian's waist as they walked through the beautiful corridors of his parents' house. They approached the door to the conservatory and Nick bent over and placed a kiss on her cheek before opening the door for her.

"Lillian, darling, how lovely to see you," Victoria stated, getting up from her seat, placing a kiss on each cheek.

"Good morning, Victoria. I wish we were here under different circumstances, but it is lovely to see you," Lillian responded looking over to Steve.

Victoria nodded in understanding. "Well, if you would like to come over for tea at some point, you are always welcome. Just send me a message and we shall get something organised."

"Thank you very much. I would like that immensely," Lillian replied as she watched Nick give his mother a peck on each cheek in greeting.

Steve was sitting at the end of the table, book in hand as the two approached.

"Morning lovebirds," he said, not looking up from his book.

"Morning Mr Madden," Lillian said, taking a seat beside him.

"My dear, I told you, call me Steve," he replied, raising an eyebrow but still not looking up from his reading.

"With all due respect sir. I'd prefer to stay formal when we meet for work purposes and call you by your given name when we are meeting up outside of that," she said folding her hands together on top of the table.

He slowly looked up from his book, closing the cover and placing it down and smiled at the girl sitting in front of him.

"Of course, Miss Robertson. Shall we retire to my office then to conduct this meeting," he asked, his tone turning formal.

Lillian looked at Nick and smiled, reassuring him. "That sounds like a good idea," she responded.

The three of them stood up and walked into the office, Lillian giving a small wave and smile to Victoria before entering the dark room that was Steve's office. She looked around, admiring the bookshelves that lined the room. There was a lit fire behind him, that took up the majority of the wall and a large window with stunning views of the mountains on another wall. Just past the window was a balcony and on the balcony was a little bird, its head tilted to the side. Lillian went to take a step towards the window when Steve suddenly spoke.

"Please have a seat," Steve said, indicating the plush seats directly opposite his. "So have you had time to think and have a couple of days to trial out the new position," he said, looking at Lillian.

She nodded. "Yes sir. I had three days where I practiced the magic and managed to bring you a few of the people that the magic told me to," she replied, her voice steady and unfaltering.

Nick looked at her shocked. Of course he'd seen the way she'd arrived home but hadn't even thought about how she got in that state. He was meant to be protecting her and was doing an extremely poor job of it.

Lillian looked over at him, feeling the effects of his emotional turmoil hit her like a brick. She reached out and grabbed his hand, rubbing her thumb gently across his knuckles.

"It's okay," she said quietly so only Nick could hear.

She turned to Steve. "I need more practice, but I managed two out of three of them easily. The magic itself was simple enough to control and the third, I ended up using some of the elemental magic I've been practicing on and he then came easy enough after that," she said shrugging. "However, I think I need to get in better physical shape and practice more. Also having Nick around will be helpful too as he is more experienced with magic than I am."

She smiled at Nick and then looked back at his father who was watching them intently.

"You have done incredibly well, my dear. With so little training as well. It's amazing what your brain is capable of with just a bit of literature in front of it. I have some more books for you, but I'm sure your mother would appreciate some company today," he said, looking towards Nick with his eyebrow arched.

Nick stared at his father and shook his head at him after a few moments. "Please tell me you are joking?" Nick mumbled.

"Speak clearly son," his father said, standing up and patting him on the back.

"Bastard," he muttered, as his father left the room chuckling.

Nick turned to Lillian, his eyes wide. "I'm so sorry. I didn't know…" he said, pleading with Lillian. She took his hands in his eyes and tried to calm him down.

"Hey, what's up?" she responded, smiling sweetly at him.

"My grandparents are coming today," he said looking at the ground.

Lillian's smile faltered but she got it under control. "So we've been tricked here today then? Your father didn't really want updates then?" she asked as Nick shook his head.

Lillian sighed and then her eyes grew wide. "I'm meeting the king and queen today?" she asked, jumping up from her seat.

"It's okay. Lillian, everything will be okay," Nick said, standing up and taking her hand.

"How do I address them? Do I wait until they've spoken to me? Am I allowed to speak to them at all?" She started to hyperventilate and pace around the room in circles.

"Love, calm down. It's just my grandparents. Nothing more. You are meeting my family today. That is it. Calm down," he said, kissing her temple.

Lillian took a calming breath, inhaling deeply. "Okay, I can do this," she said, standing up proudly.

"Let's do this," Nick said, beaming at her, reaching his hand out to grasp hers.

They walked through Nick's childhood home to the gardens out the back. Victoria and Steve were sitting on the bench overlooking the entire garden.

"Nick, Lillian, come take a seat," Victoria said, patting the bench next to her.

Lillian smiled at Nick and skipped over to Victoria. Nick stopped walking and laughed as he watched Lillian skip over to his mother and start chatting away to her. Steve looked up from his paper and shook his head, smiling a little bit, before his eyes darted down to his paper again.

Nick heard a noise coming from behind him and spun around on the spot.

"Grandmother! Grandfather! How lovely to see you," he said, kissing his grandmother on the cheek and shaking his grandfather's hand. This caught Lillian's attention and all the colour drained from her face.

She quickly stood up as Victoria whispered, "Relax."

"This is Lillian," Nick said as Lillian walked over towards him.

"Your majesties," Lillian said, curtseying.

Nick's grandfather laughed out loud, a cheerful laugh that came from the bottom of his belly.

"I like this one, Nicky boy. She's funny!" he said, clapping Nick on the back. He turned to Lillian and smiled at her. "None of these niceties, my dear. Just call me Francis and this beautiful lady here is Regina." Lillian smiled and shook Francis' hand and turned to Regina who refused to look at her.

"Mother," Victoria said, in a warning tone. "Don't you worry. I have vetted her and she is perfect for Nick. They are twin flames, just ignore our heritage for once in our life and meet the love of his life please," Victoria said, placing a hand supportively on Lillian's shoulder.

Lillian smiled at Victoria appreciatively.

Regina turned to Nick. "Why was it up to your mother to defend your supposed love?" she said, looking him square in the eye.

Nick sighed, in shock and ran a hand through his hair. "I was never going to win here, was I?"

Lillian laughed. "You should know by now, when your mother and I are together you don't stand a chance, never mind when we add your grandmother into the mix," she said, cheekily sticking her tongue out at him.

He crossed his arms over his chest and tried hard to keep the scowl on his face, despite wanting to laugh at the interaction between the three most important women in his life.

"It's a pleasure to meet you, my dear, Nicky here, he talks very highly of you," Regina said, taking a seat next to Lillian.

Mrs Miller appeared at this point with a tea set for them all and poured each of them a cup of tea, just the way they liked it as they sat in the mid afternoon sun, enjoying each other's company.

Chapter Fifteen

"Hey, sir, can I speak to you wherever you have a minute?" Lillian said when she got into work. Her boss was an angry man, that was three times the size of her and she was nervous to say the least.

"Come on Lillian. Take a seat, we will get this sorted now so that we can actually get some work done tonight," he sneered, before storming off in the other direction.

She followed slowly behind him, taking a deep breath and passing the bit of paper between her hands nervously.

He sat, staring at her as she approached. She pulled the chair out slowly and sat down opposite him.

"This is for you," she said, sliding the bit of paper across the table. He took it and unfolded the paper, scowling in the process.

To whom it may concern,

Please accept this letter as formal notification of my intention to resign from my position as a waitress with this company. In accordance with my notice period, my final day will be next Tuesday.

I would like to thank you for the opportunity to have worked in the position for the past five years. I have learned a great deal during my time here and have enjoyed collaborating with my colleagues. I will take a lot of what I have learned with me in my career and will look back at my time here as a valuable period of my professional life.

During the next week, I will do what I can to make the transition as smooth as possible, and will support in whatever way I can to hand over my duties to colleagues or to my replacement. Please let me know if there is anything further, I can do to assist in this process.

Yours Sincerely,

Lillian Robertson

Lillian swallowed as she watched his eyes dart back and front across as he read.

"You're leaving?" he asked. She nodded her head slowly. "Well, I don't accept," he said matter-of-factly.

Lillian's eyes shot up. "What do you mean, you don't accept?" she asked.

He took the bit of paper and crumpled it up into a ball. "I don't accept. You can't leave."

Lillian was angry, she could feel the magic bubbling up inside of her and the more that she tried to stop it, the stronger it got.

She stood up, the chair flying away behind her. "You will accept it and you will file it, or I will walk out that door right now and never come back," she stated, her hands flailing about.

"Oh really?" was all her boss said, crossing his arms in front of his chest.

"Yes! Screw you," she said, turning around on the spot and leaving the building. As she walked out the door for the last time, she wiped a stray tear from her eye. It had been a terrible place to work but it had been five years of her life and they had been like a family to her when she needed them.

She wasn't paying attention to where she was going and bumped straight into Ruby.

" Hey Lil, you okay?" she said, placing a hand on her shoulder. Lillian took one look at her friend and burst into tears. Ruby wrapped her arms around Lillian.

"Come on, let's get you home," she said, turning them both around and bundling Lillian into her car.

"Ruby, you have work," Lillian said.

Ruby laughed. "Screw work. You're more important than that hell hole."

Ruby sped up to Lillian's house and the two of them walked in giggling together, the tears that Lillian had been crying forgotten in the ten-minute journey.

They walked into her living room and Ruby jumped onto her grey sofa, sending cushions flying everywhere as Lillian headed to the kitchen for a bottle of wine and two glasses.

"So, a new job?" Ruby said. "I can't believe you are leaving me behind in that hell hole. Do I get to find out what this new job is?"

Lillian sighed. "You wouldn't understand it if I told you." She downed the rest of the contents of her glass as Ruby giggled on the sofa next to her.

Two bottles of wine later, Ruby and Lillian both collapsed on the floor in hysterics. Nick appeared in the living room and looked at the two of them.

"What has happened here?" he said, leaning against the doorframe, a smirk gracing his features.

"Well, I walked out of work," Lillian started.

"And I just didn't go in since my girl needed me," Ruby finished, before starting giggling again.

Lillian took one look at Ruby and started laughing herself, so hard that tears were escaping down her face.

Nick threw himself onto a beanbag on the floor and picked up a beer from the pile of alcohol that the girls had collected and popped the lid before taking a sip.

Ruby stood up, dragging Lillian with her after another two glasses of wine. There was music playing and they started to dance around the living room together, much to Nick's amusement.

Lillian stumbled in the middle of her dancing and fell into Nick's lap. She started to giggle as he wrapped his arms around her and tickled her gently. Lillian got to the point where she couldn't breathe.

"I'm going to take this as my queue to leave," Ruby said, giggling as she attempted to stand up. She collapsed into a heap on the floor. "Or I may sleep here…" She started to giggle uncontrollably.

Nick stood up, scooping Lillian up in his arms and placing a tender kiss on her lips. "My beautiful lady…" he said, as Ruby giggled in the background.

Nick appeared at Ruby's side the next morning with a glass of water.

"Drink this," he said as Lillian appeared at his side looking worse for wear. "Morning sunshine," he said laughing.

Lillian collapsed on the spot next to Ruby and hid her head in the crook of her friend's shoulder. "I feel like death," she whimpered.

Ruby laughed, then held her hand from the pain that shot through her. head.

"Come on guys. I've made you a hangover cure, including eggs, bacon and other greasy things," he said as he ran a hand through his messy, tousled hair.

The girls made eye contact and helped each other get up, Ruby winking at Lillian.

"You got yourself a good one there," she whispered, elbowing Lillian in the side. "Has he got a brother?"

Nick laughed. "No I don't but I do have a handsome cousin that I can set you up with," he said wrapping his arm around Lillian's shoulders, kissing her temple.

"Oh, please tell me more. You have to set that up," Ruby said, giggling.

Lillian laughed as she took a sip of the coffee that Nick put in front of her.

"Ruby, what are you going to do about work? He's going to be so pissed about last night."

Ruby looked at her plate and moved the food around it with her fork.

"I'll find something. Without you there, it would be no fun," she said, taking a sip of her coffee. "Hey, what about you? Can I come work with you?"

Lillian choked on her drink as Nick gently hit her back. "Erm, no. I don't think that would be a good idea. I'm sorry," Lillian said.

"Wait no! I could get something sorted for you," Nick said, stopping suddenly, a smile spreading across his face. Lillian looked at him confused.

"Really?" Ruby said, her voice rising with excitement.

"Yeah, just give me a few hours and I will see what I can get sorted for you," Nick said, sending a wink in Lillian's direction as he grabbed his coat and disappeared into the morning light.

Chapter Sixteen

Lillian knocked on the now familiar door. Julius opened and smiled down at her, his eyes twinkling through the lenses of his glasses.

"Hello, my dear. I'm so glad you could come today. I have prepared tea for us," he said as he walked to the small table he had set up in the middle of the room. He took the teapot and poured the steaming tea into two cups and made each one just as they liked it.

Lillian accepted the cup as she shrugged her jacket off, laying it gently on the back of the chair. She inhaled the scent deeply, the warmth filling her with happiness.

"So, what would you like to study today?" Julius asked, as he sat opposite her, crossing his legs in front of himself.

"I was thinking that we could carry on with the rituals of *Necromancy* today. I feel like we are finally getting somewhere," she said, before taking a large sip of her tea.

"That we are, my dear," Julius declared, before he also took a large drink of his tea, his glasses steaming up in the process.

They sat in comfortable silence whilst they finished their drinks. As soon as they put the cups down, Lillian headed to her usual spot, over beside the window and Julius got up and started pacing the room, heading over to one of the many bookshelves and quickly reading different spines until he found the one that he was looking for.

"The processing of such a complex topic as the *necromantic* manipulation of the dead can be a difficult task to accomplish, especially if the facts provided by history are often vague and based in the realm of myths and legends," Julius explained as Lillian sat at her window seat, looking out over the grounds. "It is very much a learning curve; you get shown the basics and it depends on your magical ability and motivation on how well you can achieve results."

Lillian opened the window as Julius spoke and the little robin appeared, fluttering in and landing on Lillian's knee. She patted it gently on the head as she listened to Julius as he walked around the room.

"The Oracles of the Dead were known under many different names in the Antiquity, but their meaning was approximately the same — a place where one could communicate with the dead. If you want to do this, then you must find somewhere that you feel safe and comfortable to do so. Somewhere that you are connected with the spirits," Julius started, picking up a book and placing it in front of her. "The ritual itself involved the consumption of several meals prepared for this occasion, an offering to Hades and Persephone, the ritual of burning something belonging to the dead with whom you wish to communicate and purification of oneself after which the consultor would fall into a sleep during which he would encounter the dead in their dreams."

Julius stopped wandering around the room and picked up another book. He flipped through a few pages, before starting to read again. "According to tradition, souls can be found loitering around their gravesite for up to a year after interment above or below ground. However, this is far from a steadfast rule. Still, some accounts would suggest that, after only a few hundred days, it tends to become increasingly more difficult to communicate with the departed the longer they have been deceased. This is why *necromancers* have to put in a lot of work scouting out perfect locations and victims based on specific times and places, always on the hunt for the recently deceased. As part of this, necromancers prefer to work in certain kinds of places like inside mausoleums and vaults, deep in forest glens, in abandoned monasteries, or even at the corners of crossroads, to name but a few of the more ideal locations. This might be difficult depending on who it is you want to communicate with, but I have faith in you and your magic child," Julius stated, looking up through his glasses and smiling at her.

Lillian nodded her head and picked up her notebook, writing down a few notes and working out where the best place to achieve the results she needed and wanted were.

"Your mother would be so very proud of you, you know," he said, placing his hand on her shoulder and stroking the robin very gently.

"So," Lillian started, ignoring Julius' previous comment. "I'm essentially doing a sleep-induced seance, bribing the Greek gods and will be hallucinating, seeing the person that I am speaking to…"

"Essentially, yes," Julius said, before looking back at the book. "In general, *necromancers* also tend to prefer to mainly work in the dark, such as very late at night or early in the morning. To be more precise, during a new moon, after midnight, usually between one and three a.m. is about the best time to divine with the dead. Then again, a tempestuous night of rainstorms can also set the scene even better. Either way, most *necromancers* tend to believe that the dead are more easily revealed in these ideal conditions."

Julius walked back over to Lillian and placed the book in front of her. "Here is one of the spells that you can use and how to create them. Write it down. Regardless of how it's done, once a spirit is made to appear and compelled to obedience, many *necromancers* will coerce cooperation out of them by forming a pact. They assure the dead that they will go undisturbed in the future, telling them that they will either burn their body or bury it. This way, the deceased would know that their corpse would be gone, so the soul could never be called back to it again."

Lillian scribbled down notes. The spell seemed easy enough. Create a statement of intent. Remove the repeating letters. Rearrange the letters that are left. Chant the words that are now created in an exaggerated style.

As Lillian put the lid on her pen, the robin chirped before flying away.

"I think that's a sign that I need to leave too," she said, laughing as she watched it fly out into the garden. "Thank you so much for today, Julius." He nodded his head as she handed him the books back that she had placed around her.

"No problem, my dear. I'm here any time. Oh, did I tell you I heard from my friend, Rodney?"

Lillian smiled. She loved hearing about Rodney's adventures. She wasn't sure if he was real or a figment of Julius' imagination, but she loved to listen anyway. "Oh? How is he?" she asked.

"He's doing well. His wife has just had babies. Twins!" he responded, clapping his hands excitedly.

"Amazing! Next time you hear from him, please say congratulations from me," she said, putting her coat on.

"Actually dear, I am planning on going to see them soon, so I can tell him in person," he said, placing the books back on the shelves.

"That will be so nice for you. Thank you again Julius," Lillian said as she waved at him before disappearing from sight, leaving a dark shadow in her wake.

"Interesting…" Julius muttered, going to his desk and grabbing his journal. *Lillian is nearly there… She is prepared. There is not much more I can do to help the girl. A dark shadow is following her. She is ready…*

Chapter Seventeen

Lillian and Nick sat on the hill overlooking the city.

"Dawn of a new day…" Lillian stated, resting her head against Nick's shoulder.

"So quiet. Watching a sunrise means you get to experience the quiet before the hustle and bustle of people's energy and the waking world. The silence is bliss," Nick said, stroking Lillian's hair as they watched the sun come up.

Lillian sighed contently as she admired the sky changing colour in front of her. Nick handed her a flask of hot chocolate which she sipped at, embracing the warmth.

"I needed this," she whispered, as she slowly stood up from the cold ground.

"Me too. I hate my father you know," he said, taking her hand as he stood up as well.

"I know," she said, caressing his cheek before threading her fingers through his hair and bringing his lips down to hers. The kiss was simple, a basic declaration of their feelings.

"Nick, I need to tell you something," Lillian started, but he held his finger up to her lips, hushing her in the process.

"I love you," he said, looking her directly in the eye, caressing her cheek softly.

She smiled happily, tears welling in her eyes. "I love you too," she said kissing him soundly in the lips, lost in the moment.

They separated and he wrapped his arms around her waist, pulling her close to him.

"I hate to break this up, but we have to go…" she said, dancing her fingers across his arm. He hummed in approval and placed kisses on her neck.

"Come on then," he mumbled into her skin, not wanting to break the happiness they were feeling in the moment.

She grabbed his hand and pulled him away. They entwined their fingers and she focused on finding the location that they were heading. She closed her eyes and lights flickered behind her lids. "I know where we are going," she said, pulling on his arm lightly. "You ready?"

Nick laughed as she pulled on him again, focusing all her magic on the two of them as they vanished from the spot they were in, leaving behind a dark shadow.

They arrived in an old derelict building. She looked at the cracked windows and saw the pattern of sunlight streaming in, leaving a design on the floors and walls.

"It's here," Nick said quietly, grabbing her head tighter as they headed towards the stairs, his eyes flaring the brightest green she had ever seen.

With each step they took, the stairs creaked a little louder.

"Let me go in first," Nick said quietly, stopping Lillian from getting past him.

Lillian sighed and moved him out of the way. "It's my fault we're doing this at all," she said. "Please let me go in first?"

Nick raked his hand through his hair and sighed. She was stubborn but right and he knew he would never live a peaceful life if he didn't agree.

"Okay, but I'll be right behind you," he said, touching her wrist lovingly.

"I know," she said, kissing his cheek chastely.

She slowly opened the door and sighed at the sight before her. The door creaked announcing her presence and a pair of silver eyes looked up and met hers.

"You're here for me," the frail wizard stated "About bloody time." He let out a chortle and started to push himself out of the bed he was curled in.

"Mr Watkins, are you ready?" she asked, approaching him. She held out her elbow and helped him up.

"I've been ready for years," he stated grabbing his hat on the way out of the door. "There's two of you. Did he think that I was going to put up a fight?" He let out a throaty chuckle again.

Lillian smiled at him as she walked past Nick. "I got this. I'll meet you at home," she said, kissing him on the cheek before vanishing, once again leaving a dark shadow in her wake.

Nick smiled to himself. That wasn't too bad. She was safe. One down, a lifetime to go.

Chapter Eighteen

Lillian sat on the sofa curled up, cup of tea in her hand, Ruby sat opposite her. They were giggling away when Nick walked in.

"Ladies," he said, bowing slightly at their presence.

Ruby giggled as Nick walked over and kissed Lillian on the cheek. "I have some news," he said as he shrugged off his coat.

Lillian looked up at this as he came to sit beside her, wrapping an arm around her shoulders.

"So Ruby, how would you like an administrative role at my father's company? No interview required as I vouched for you. Decent pay, nice rewards, your own office…" he trailed off handing her some paperwork.

Ruby scanned over the documents quickly and a huge smile broke out over her face.

"Really?" she asked, bouncing up and down on the spot with excitement.

"Really," he responded.

She lunged forward and wrapped him and Lillian in a giant bear hug. "Thank you so much," she said, wiping a stray happy tear from her eye.

Nick smiled at her as she untangled herself from him. "Honestly, it was nothing," he said, nonchalantly. "My father needs the help, even if he won't admit it. Hours aren't always the best though."

Ruby shrugged. "I used to work night shift... I can deal with some irregular hours."

Lillian interlinked Nick's fingers with her own. "I think this calls for a celebration," Lillian said, smiling at Ruby. "How about a takeaway and a sleepover. We can gossip, watch trashy movies and drink gin until stupid o'clock in the morning?"

Nick chuckled at the girls who started to excitedly plan out their night.

"I'll join you girls for the takeaway then leave you to it. I think it's time you two spent some time together outside of work," he said, rubbing his thumb gently over Lillian's knuckles, she turned to him and mouthed a quick 'thank you' before her attention landed back on Ruby. They decided on Italian for food.

When the food arrived, they all sat on the floor to eat it and put on some rubbish film about vampires on the TV to watch.

Nick said goodbye not long after they had finished and he had tidied up any dishes that were left lying about but not before he had kissed Lillian on the cheek.

Ruby sat grinning at Lillian.

"What?" she asked, throwing a pillow at Ruby.

"You love him," she stated, matter-of-factly.

Lillian grinned. "Just a little bit."

Ruby squealed in excitement. "You landed on your feet there."

Lillian smiled brightly. "I know."

Lillian stood up, going to the kitchen and grabbing a bottle of tequila. She walked back through to Ruby, shaking the bottle at her.

"Interested?" she asked, smirking at her friend.

Ruby stood up, grabbing the bottle, uncorking it and taking a swig before responding, "Always."

Half a bottle of tequila later, Ruby and Lillian were in crumbled up heap on the floor, giggling away.

"So, I have to ask," Ruby slurred, giggling as she said it. "How's the S.E.X?" She spelled it out before dissolving into a fit of giggles.

Lillian burst out laughing. "You are incorrigible... But amazing!"

Ruby started sniggering. "And?" She held up her hand, indicating a size.

"*Ruby*!" Lillian cried out, her face blazing red in embarrassment.

"I'm just curious," she said, taking the bottle and handing it to Lillian.

Lillian took another swig before reaching across and placing Ruby's hands a certain distance apart, before dissolving into giggles again.

Ruby's eyes went wide before she muttered, "Lucky girl."

It wasn't too much longer before the two of them passed out on a heap on the floor.

The next morning, Lillian woke with a blinding headache and Nick stood over her, holding two cups of coffee. One for her and one for Ruby.

"It's from that cafe we went to. It has a hangover cure in it. Drink it," he said, helping her sit up, before doing the same to Ruby.

"You both need to drink up, then Lillian you are going to take Ruby away for a shower and give her some clothes as we have a lunch date…" He quirked his eyebrow in their direction as realisation came over them both.

"Your cousin?" Ruby exclaimed, the loud noise hurting her head. She took a sip of coffee and her headache started to ease off. "Whatever this is Nick, I need you to bring me one every time I drink, please?"

Nick chuckled as he watched the girls down their coffees and scramble up the stairs to get ready.

"What am I going to do with them," he mumbled to himself, before starting to tidy up the mess in the living room.

As Ruby came out of the shower, Lillian was already dressed and had a pile of clothes laid out on the bed. "For you, Mon Cheri," she said, indicating the many different outfits.

Ruby looked at the huge pile and sighed, sitting herself down on the edge of the bed. "Lils, I'm so nervous," Ruby uttered.

"You'll be absolutely fine," she said, taking a seat next to her best friend and placing a hand on her knee. "He's going to love you and if he doesn't it's his loss. Now get dressed." Lillian stood up and left the bedroom, wanting to go find Nick and spend some time cuddled up in his arms before they left.

She walked into a now spotless living room and smiled as she saw him reclining on the sofa. She popped herself down next to him, tucking herself under his arm and snuggled down close.

"You girls okay?" he asked, not opening his eyes.

Lillian made a noise of agreement and snuggled down closer, waiting for Ruby to be ready.

There was a knock at the door and Nick untangled himself from Lillian as he got up to answer.

"Tristan!" he exclaimed, bringing him in for a one shoulder hug. "Long time, no see buddy." Lillian watched as the two reacquainted themselves, standing awkwardly beside the sofa.

"This is the beautiful and wonderful Lillian," Nick stated, wrapping an arm around her waist as he walked over to her.

"Pleasure," Lillian said, shaking Tristan's hand.

"I've heard so much about you," he said, smiling broadly.

"All good I hope," she said, smirking up at Nick.

Tristan laughed. "Only the best I assure you."

A soft clicking of heels on the stairs had them all turning their attention to Ruby.

"You boys stay here, I'll go get her," Lillian said, excusing herself.

She looked stunning.

"Woah girl, you look amazing. That dress… wow!" Lillian said as Ruby entered the room.

"I can change. I feel ridiculous" Ruby said, playing with her hands in front of her.

"Don't. You. Dare!" Lillian commanded, before turning round on the spot and pulling Ruby along with her.

Lillian pulled Ruby along with her to the living room where Tristan and Nick were now sitting on the sofa.

Lillian cleared her throat and two pairs of emerald, green eyes, twinkled in her direction.

His hair was worn in a casual, tousled look, although Ruby suspected he spent a fair bit of time getting it to look as though he'd hadn't given it a second thought. He was also carrying a small, but stunning, bouquet of expensive magical roses which changed colour depending on people's moods. Ruby took them and sent a small smile Tristan's way.

"Thank you," she quietly said, as she turned and handed them to Lillian, unsure of where to put them.

Hurrying into the kitchen with the roses, Lillian summoned her best vase and magically arranged the bouquet. Settling the flowers on her kitchen windowsill, she smiled as she looked at the beautiful display.

Two arms wound round her waist and Nick placed his head on her shoulder.

"I didn't think you'd like flowers, or I would have brought you some myself," he whispered into her ear, making her shiver.

"I don't but these are exceptional," she responded, turning around in Nick's embrace. "I don't need gifts anyway. Just being able to spend time with you is enough."

She reached up on her tiptoes and placed a delicate kiss on his lips.

A crash came from the living room and they quickly walked through to see what had happened.

"I'm sorry you feel that way. I thought I saw something in you, but clearly, I was wrong," Tristan said.

"What? Saw what?" Ruby shouted, picking up her other shoe and throwing it at him.

"That night at the club. I thought that maybe… Maybe the past was in the past, but it doesn't matter. I don't expect you to understand… I am sorry… about the way I acted. It was unacceptable," he said, looking up and locking eyes with Nick.

A silent 'oh', escaped Nick's lips as he looked at Ruby and Tristan, his eyebrows furrowed.

"What is going on?" Lillian demanded, crossing her arms and tapping her foot. "Ruby, put down the shoe. No! I don't want to hear it… Come with me."

Ruby was away to interrupt when Lillian stopped and sent her a glare. "No arguing. Now!"

Ruby fell into line and followed her friend back out of the room.

"I'm sorry," Ruby said, sitting on the bed and resting her head in her hands.

"Hey, it's okay. But you have to talk to me. What's going on?" Lillian asked as she sat next to her friend.

"We dated. A while back and he stopped calling and texting and just started ignoring me… I haven't been on a date since," Ruby explained, crossing her legs in front of her.

Lillian sighed and sat down next to her.

"I remember how it affected you. But now is the time to get closure," Lillian said, taking Ruby's hands in hers. "Tell him how much he hurt you. This is a chance not many people get."

Ruby looked up at Lillian, a few unshed tears in her eyes, and Lillian wrapped her arms around her. "You stay here. I'll go speak to him while you freshen yourself up."

Lillian walked down the stairs, her hands on her hips.

"Tristan... What the actual hell?" Lillian angrily shouted as she approached.

"Uh oh... That's her scary voice," Nick laughed. "You're in trouble!" He poked Tristan in the ribs.

Lillian rounded on Nick. "Don't you start!" she said pointing at his chest. "You!" She turned back to face Tristan. "Don't you turn those Madden eyes on me. You explain to me what you did to that girl upstairs. Right now."

Tristan looked at her with a confused expression crossing his face, tiny little dimples forming as he pursed his lips together. "I don't know what she thinks happened," he said, frowning.

"I know exactly what happened," Ruby said from behind them. "We got serious too quickly. You blew me off. Simple." Ruby shrugged as she walked over and picked her shoes up and started to put them on.

"What do you mean I blew you off? You're the one who stopped returning my calls?" Tristan said, taking his phone out of his pocket and turning it round to show her his call log.

"Wait, what?" Lillian asked, walking over and looking at his phone. "Ruby, I love you but you're an idiot and owe Tristan an apology." She laughed out loud.

"Lils!" Ruby scowled, crossing her arms across her chest.

Lillian laughed again. "Ruby, when did you get your new phone?" she asked, walking over to Nick and wrapping herself up in his arms.

Realisation dawned over Ruby's face. "My God. It was my fault!" She turned on the spot to face Tristan. "I'm so sorry! This really is all my fault. Can we maybe try again? Try again with the realisation that I'm a freaking idiot," she said, her face turning red with embarrassment.

"So, dinner?" Lillian asked the room, noticing the time and thinking that her stomach was feeling rather empty. Nick nodded but when the two of them looked at the other side of the room, they noticed that Ruby and Tristan were in a bubble of their own.

Tristan felt his hand move to her face, brushing a stray hair off her cheek. She closed her eyes, knowing what was coming next. She was right. She felt his lips brush against hers, so gently. He pulled away before she could react, causing her to open her eyes. She saw him in front of her face, looking into her eyes, questioning whether it was okay. She reached her hand up to his neck, standing on her toes to make it easier, and brought their lips together. This time, the kiss was more than a gentle pressing together of their lips.

"Okay," Lillian said again. "Dinner?"

Ruby looked up from her spot in Tristan's arms, a huge smile beaming across her face as she nodded in agreement.

The four of them walked outside and bundled into Nick's car and headed into the city centre.

"Where the hell are we going?" Lillian asked as Nick pulled into a parking space in an area she didn't know.

"For food and a surprise," Nick said, taking her hand and pulling her along.

They walked into a large shopping complex, with shops and restaurants and bars and a large neon sign at the end of the building.

"We are going bowling?" Lillian asked, jumping up and down with excitement.

"Yep, and to eat and drink some cocktails. To treat you girls," Tristan said, wrapping his leather clad arm around Ruby's shoulders.

They walked over to the bar, placed some orders for drinks and headed over to the bowling alley. The sound of the ball hitting the pins resounded in Lillian's ears and made her smile, thinking of times she had been bowling with her mother.

The drinks arrived and they all took their shot at bowling. The match was ridiculously close and Lillian and Nick were tied in first place in the last round.

Lillian won and it was Ruby's turn to buy drinks, so they headed up to the bar and as they waited for their drinks, Lillian and Ruby started to dance.

The boys watched from their seats and Nick smirked at Tristan.

"We did good mate," he said, elbowing him in the ribs.

Tristan nodded his eyes never leaving Ruby dancing. The girls walked back with drinks and Lillian threw herself into Nick's lap, giggling as she did so.

"Tristan was totally checking you out, Ruby," Nick said, earning a glare from Tristan.

"Were you?" Ruby asked, hoping she would get the answer she wanted.

"Was I? What? Drooling over you? Absolutely," he said, honestly.

"Why?" she asked.

"You are sexy as fuck. You were so free and dancing around like you don't have a care in the world. But you know what? I'm a hot-blooded man and I know what I like when I see it," Tristan said.

"That's very... honest of you," she said, taking a large swig of her drink.

Lillian and Nick exchanged a look.

The two couples ended up in their own little bubbles, both exchanging kisses and soft caresses in between shots of bowling, until the girls were struggling to stand up to bowl.

"So, will you go out with me again?" Tristan asked a tipsy Ruby.

Ruby hesitated. "I'm... I don't... My brain hurts," she exclaimed.

"Well, text me when you figure all this out. I'm in, Ruby. I want to be with you. I did the first time and I do now. You just need to figure out if you want the same," he said.

149

Ruby looked at him with no indication that she knew what to say.

"People will see us together. That's a given. People will talk. Your ex will talk. I'm always going to be me and you're always going to be you. What you need to decide is if you can get past all that and allow yourself to be happy, for the first time in forever," he said, looking at her eagerly for a response.

"I…" she said, but stopped when she realised she had no idea what to say… still.

Tristan simply turned and walked away, exiting the building via the front door, leaving Ruby standing alone, gawking at his retreating form.

"What did I just do?" Ruby asked, looking between Lillian and Nick.

Nick just shrugged his shoulders. "Let's get you girls home."

Chapter Nineteen

"Lillian, are you ready?" Nick asked, as he took her hand.

She took another look at herself in the mirror. The robe she had on was floor-length and dark velvet with a satin lined hood.

"I'm ready," she said, grabbing his hand before disappearing away from the house in a puff of magic.

They landed with a thump in a short, steep glen. In front of them was a rock formation that looked like a church pulpit. In front of them was an emerald cavern, with crimson water and blood-red waterfalls all around. It was like something out of a magical fairy tale.

"Where are we?" Nick asked, looking around at the beautiful setting.

"About thirty minutes outside of Glasgow..." Lillian replied, bending down and running her hands through the water.

"The Devil's Pulpit," Nick stated, looking round in admiration. "It's exactly like I imagined it."

"And the perfect place to request to speak to the dead," Lillian finished.

Nick smirked at her, an eyebrow raising in amusement. It was a very clever move on Lillian's part to find this place to hold her ritual.

Lillian looked down at her hands and nervously started to play with the sleeve of her robe.

"Lils, you have this. You've done all the research and practised. Don't doubt yourself," Nick said, as he wrapped his arms around her.

Heat rose from Lillian's stomach to her chest. Nick's lips were getting closer and her heart decided to skip a beat, the smell of him hypnotic beyond reason. She parted her lips and felt him washing over like a wave of warmth, curling her toes, unfurling all her senses as the taste of him nearly silenced all thoughts. Until she remembered where she was and the reason behind her being there.

"I'm ready," she said, stepping away from his embrace.

"You will rock this," Nick said, kissing her knuckles briefly.

"Thank you for being here today. You have no idea how much it means to me," she said, dropping his hand and turning to where she needed to be.

Lillian walked to the centre of the river, where the rock formation came out of the water and stood, a vision of beauty as she started to perform her ritual. She stood in the spot that Hades had once stood, addressing his followers, asking him to grant her request, the crimson current swirling at her feet.

She looked around at her surroundings, smiling to herself. The soft crunch of the leaves on the ground made her wistful. They were a faded, shredded tapestry of autumn, she thought as she remembered the crisp golden hues and the vibrant oranges that had blanketed the forest floor. The trees were ancient, timeless as they disappeared into the sky, rough with age, yet their roughness had been worn down by the soft greenness of moss that had slowly made them home. Some trees were wreathed in ivy, ever frozen in its embrace, whilst others were still bare; young shoots that hadn't enough time to have claimed companions. In the canopy above, birds twittered, chirping and calling in distant melodies to their kin. A faint rustling could be heard as small rodents scampered through the foliage, though it was drowned out by the gushing river.

She bent down and placed her hands in the water "*Spotka merdh. Spotka merdh. Spotka merdh*!" she chanted, running her hands through the water and lifting the cool liquid up and letting it run down her body.

The wind slowly started to pick up and the leaves around them rustled. The water started to pick up speed and waves started to splash at Lillian's feet. As she stood up, she placed her hands above her head, reaching up to the sky, feeling the wind rush around her wet skin.

"*Spotka merdh*!" Lillian continued to chant as the elements wrapped around her, lifting her up into the air. The magic swirled around her, wrapping her in a blanket of energy.

"*Spotka merdh! Spotka merdh! Spotka merdh*!"

The magic shot out from the tips of her fingers and the bottom of her feet, shooting out into the sky, her hair wrapping up into the breeze.

Nick stood staring at her, his mouth open in shock. She looked like an angel floating in the middle of the glen. Everything stood still, apart from her in this moment, all time stopped as he watched her in her element. From the rich brown earthen hues of the forest ground to the sweetness of the blue-white sky and the scarlet water running beneath her feet, the contrast of the colours brightened for him in this moment. Rays of mellow sunlight filtered through the verdurous canopy, penetrating through the leaves and casting an unearthly green-gold luminescence over the ground.

All of a sudden, the elements stopped all around her and Nick watched as Lillian collapsed into a heap on the floor. He went running over to her.

"Lillian… Lillian!" he called out as he threw himself in the water beside her. "Lillian, talk to me!"

"It didn't work…" She cried, clutching at Nick's shirt, burying her face in his chest.

He lifted her up and carried her out of the water, her sobbing body shaking against him. "It didn't work." She cried over and over again.

Nick kept one hand under her legs and rubbed soothing circles on her back.

"It's okay," he said, focusing all his attention on his home as he transported them there, his arms wrapped securely around her.

He laid her down on the sofa gently as he went to run a hot bath for her. He poured her favourite bubbles in it and waited for the water to fill up the tub. Once it was full and the water had stopped, he went back to the living room and picked up the still sobbing Lillian. He carried her to the bathroom and gently placed her into the water.

Gently, he washed her, warming her with the hot, soapy water, he slowly washed her hair, tying it up.

"Why didn't it work? I tried so damn hard. I practised and researched so much. It should have worked." She rubbed the tears out of her eyes. "I don't understand."

"I know," Nick said, once again, rubbing soothing circles on her back. "We can try again. Whenever you want. This is all up to you."

Lillian swallowed hard. "I don't want to…" She sighed.

"Lils, you worked so har…"

"I know, Nick!" she snapped. "I did work hard. Just leave me alone for now. Please?"

Nick stood up and placed a kiss softly on her forehead before leaving the room, shutting the door gently behind him, understanding that she needed some alone time.

Chapter Twenty

Lillian curled up on the bed, her head laid on Nick's chest as he read a book, every now and again reading out loud. "I have two things I wanted to discuss with you," Lillian said, suddenly sitting upright.

Nick looked at her, putting his book down and running a hand through his hair. "Okay, but only if I get to ask you something in exchange," he said, smirking at her.

She laughed as she leaned forward and captured his lips in a sweet kiss.

"Okay, you go first?" Nick said, pulling her in close and playing with a stray strand of her hair.

"So, first question. When was the last time you did a live stream? I'm lucky I get to spend all this time with you, but I know other people would worry," Lillian said as she threaded her hand together with Nick's.

He thought for a moment. "Hmm. That's a good point. The last one I did would probably have been when I debuted my song. It's been far too long. I might do one later tonight. I can't help the fact that I've been distracted." Nick smirked, obviously pleased with himself and lowered his head and his lips met Lillian's. He kissed her hungrily, making her gasp at his aggressiveness. She closed her eyes and melted into his arms.

They pulled apart several moments later and Lillian giggled. "This is why we never get anything done," she stated. "I believe it was you turn to ask me a question."

Nick sighed, gathering her up into his arms and placing a chaste kiss on her lips before speaking. "I just wanted to ask. Are you okay? We haven't spoken about what happened at the Glen and I just wanted to make sure you were good."

Lillian reached up and pushed Nick's hair out of his face. "You want an honest answer?"

Nick nodded his head, resting his cheek on her shoulder as he hugged her tightly to him.

"No, I'm completely devastated that it didn't work. I'm confused as to why it didn't work. Does it mean I did something wrong? Am I not powerful enough? Am I stupid for even considering that I could manage?" She sniffled as she ranted, "I just want to talk to my mum. Let her know I'm okay."

Nick stroked a hand through her hair. "I know," he whispered, gently kissing the crown of her head.

They sat there as Lillian quietly sobbed, the grief of not being able to contact her mother washing over her again.

She sat up and looked out the window. "It's snowing!" she exclaimed. The flakes drifted directly down, undisturbed in their descent by any hint of a breeze in the still night air. She walked over to the window and opened it, watching as a blanket of snow spread out before her.

She watched as her little robin friend flew towards the window, twirling through the snow, as if she were dancing with a friend. The steady downward spiral of snowflakes was mesmerising, peaceful.

Nick came over to her and ran his hands down her arms until he reached her hands, threading his fingers through hers and wrapping both their arms around her body.

"I believe you still have one more question that you wanted to ask," he whispered into her hair, before laying soft kisses along her neck.

She sighed contently, before closing the window and turning round in his embrace.

He bent down, the way his lips covered hers was consuming, hungry yet sweet, teasing her with a hint of promise and driving her body to new heights of awareness. For a moment they clung to each other, their kiss evolving from tender to eager and on to passionate.

Lillian walked Nick backwards to the bed until his knees hit the end of the mattress and they both fell onto the bed, giggling as they did.

"Okay, concentrate Lils," she said to herself, reaching up and placing a kiss on the end of his nose.

He laughed as he pulled her up the bed, placing pillows behind them to get them comfy so that they could speak once again.

"I want to know about Tristan. Is he from the royal side or the death side? Does he have ties to either? And the fact that you two look like twins is disturbing…" she rambled on.

"So if we look like twins, you must think he's good looking," Nick said, teasing her.

"He is attractive, but I can definitely see the difference and see things on you that are way more attractive than him," she said, pulling his mouth down to hers once again. This kiss was short and sweet and Nick flushed, colour rising up into his cheeks as he thought how to answer Lillian's question.

"Tristan is my cousin on my father's side, hence the dark hair and green eyes. He also works for the family business and we have a connection, one that my father does not know about. We are connected. Next time we are out working you may notice my eyes grow a little brighter and a little more colourful. This only happens when we establish this connection. I can see him and he can see me. We can make sure the other one is okay and if not then we can make sure we can help the other one out," Nick explained.

Lillian mouthed an 'oh' as she thought back and thought of the first time they had gone out on the job and his eyes had twinkled brightly. "I've seen it," she said. "That's incredible."

"In the line of work we do; it is very helpful. It's nice to have someone else looking out for me," he said, smiling and squeezing her hand. "There's more too. We have a protective familiar. It's a family pet so to say but again has the same eyes. It is a beautiful, white husky. He is loving and playful but deadly when it comes to protecting us… and now you too. You are part of this family now Lillian and as much as it excites me, it terrifies me too. I can't lose you."

"You won't lose me. I'll always be there for you. What's the husky's name?" she asked, smiling to herself. She had always wanted a dog and now she had one looking out for her.

"His name is Ghost. Ironic, huh?" Lillian couldn't hold back the laugh that erupted from her chest.

"Wait! It's only when you're working, right? That's the only time the connection can be made?" she asked, suddenly shy and self-conscious.

He nodded his head as he pulled her close and kissed her worries away. "I can turn the connection off and keep him out if I need to. Don't you worry, you are all mine!" He growled before rolling over on top of her as she giggled and squeaked in delight.

Chapter Twenty-One

"Are you sure about this?" Lillian enquired. "We can easily go home to your house with your parents for Christmas or head back to one of our flats and order takeout and never leave our bedroom?" She stood up on her tiptoes and captured his lips in a searing kiss, her hands running through his unruly hair.

"As tempting as that sounds," Nick replied, wiggling his eyebrows at Lillian. "We made a promise to your father and he is your family and I would like to meet him."

"As long as one of us does," Lillian muttered to herself.

They approached a small house, a four in a block. One garden had a burnt sofa outside the front door and the next one was missing part of the fence, had bins everywhere and rubbish blowing about the garden. The snow that had come so suddenly, had started to melt, making everything soggy and slushy underfoot. Lillian turned to look at Nick, her scarf blowing around her face.

"Welcome to the dive that I used to call home," she said as they walked down the six stones to the front door.

Lillian knocked at the door and took a step back, Nick placing his hands on her hips as they waited for her father to open the door.

The wind was bitterly cold and they stood there, waiting, watching the door as it didn't open.

Lillian walked forward, Nick following with their cases behind them. "Dad?" she said quietly as she opened the door, "Are you here?"

"Lilipad, is that you?" she heard a muffled voice call from the bedroom.

She ran through to the bedroom and saw him. She ran her hand up over her face, scrubbing the hair away from her eyes.

"Dad, what are you doing?" she said, running towards him and trying to help him out of the bed. "You're a state. You knew we were coming. It is Christmas Eve, for Christ's sake." Lillian swore as she struggled to help her dad up, a bottle of whisky falling to the ground.

Nick rushed forward and helped Lillian pick her dad up and move him to the living room.

"So, You're Nick," her Dad slurred as they threw him down on the couch, Lillian knocking documents everywhere to try and make space for him.

"Yes sir," he replied, holding his hand out to shake her father's.

"You aren't good enough for my daughter," he said, looking Nick square in the eyes.

Nick looked down at his hands and started twiddling his thumbs. Suddenly, he looked up, straight at Lillian's father, "I know that I don't," he said, speaking slowly but passionately. "But she also most definitely deserves better than this." He indicated around the room. "I understand that you have millions of things going on and that everything that happened to your wife was awful but there is no need for your daughter to come home and have to deal with this…"

Lillian looked at Nick and smiled. No one had ever stood up for her or believed in her like that and she felt so proud of the man standing by her side. "Sorry Dad, but we won't be staying. Merry Christmas," Lillian said, grabbing Nick's hand and pulling him from the house.

The two of them got to the end of the street and disappeared from sight in a puff of red smoke.

They arrived in a street, decorated with Christmas lights, snow falling from the sky, the moon highlighting everything in its path. Lillian pushed herself into him, so their bodies were against one another, pinned against the wall. Nick's breathing increased rapidly at the fact that he was this close to him, pressing her sumptuous body against his. Lillian looked into Nick's eyes that had clouded over with lust. She let her eyes wander down his face to his lips, partially opened.

Their lips met hungrily the instant her hands grabbed the front of his shirt, pulling them even closer together. Both were being driven crazy with wanting. "You have no idea how much of a turn on it was, seeing you stand up for me like that," she said between kisses.

"Mine," was all Nick said before nibbling gently on Lillian's lower lip.

Lillian pulled her head back slightly, catching her breath. "We need to go home," she said, kissing him again, this time more tenderly. "I still have your gift to give you." She sent a wink to him before starting to giggle as Nick groaned.

He wrapped his arms around her waist and huskily whispered, 'Adventure achieved', before they were transported back home.

They landed in the living room of Lillian's apartment, a giant Christmas tree towering over them with its lights twinkling. A huge fireplace cast a warm glow on the dark green Christmas fabric covering the long couch and the two armchairs, creating a cosy environment.

"I'm glad we're home," she said, pushing Nick onto the sofa before climbing into his lap. She leaned forward, capturing his lips in a searing kiss.

They slowly separated from each other, as though they never wanted to let go. His hands cupped her face, thumbs gently tracing her cheeks as he smiled down at her.

He felt her smile as she pulled him in for another breathtaking kiss, groaning as her tongue snaked its way between his lips, dancing a timeless mating dance with his. Her hands dug into his hair, pulling him closer, pressing him harder against her. His heart pounded wildly in his chest, blood heating up as desire began to rush through his veins.

"Give me a minute and I'll get your gift," she seductively said, pushing herself off of his lap and wiggling her hips as she left the room.

She quickly ran into the bathroom and changed into a slinky nightgown that was red with white fur along the hem and a large bow right in the centre.

She changed into it at rapid speed and put on a pair of ridiculous high heels before piling her hair on top of her head with a few pieces cascading down her face. She gave herself a once over in the mirror before turning and heading back to Nick in the living room.

He was laid out on her sofa, a hand resting behind his head, his eyes shut as she approached and straddled his lap. His eyes shot open, darkening at the sight of his love.

Without warning, he surged forward, pressing her against the cool glass of the wall. His lips landed on hers with a ferocity that surprised her, but then he was plundering her mouth so completely that she lost all train of thought other than pressing back against him. His hands speared into her hair, angling her head, then they began a slow slide down her body, toying with the bow at the centre of her chest.

"Best present I've ever received," he said huskily, running his hands up and down her sides, before leaning in to capture her lips.

Lillian emerged from the shower sometime later, a dressing gown wrapped tightly around her as she attempted to towel dry her curls. She looked over and saw a note on the bed. *Meet me downstairs when you're ready x*. She giggled as she chucked on a dress she had planned out for Christmas day, tartan with a little white, fluffy trim around the bottom. She slipped her feet into some little pumps and whilst looking in the mirror she focused all her energy, dipping into some air magic, on her hair. With a sparkle of silver magic, her hair was dry and in perfect ringlets. She smiled at her reflection before turning on her heel to head downstairs.

It was nearly lunchtime and her stomach gave a light rumble. "Nick?" she called out as she approached the living room.

"Kitchen," he replied. "Tea?"

"Yes please," she responded, opening the door. She was shocked at the sight before her. Nick stood in her kitchen, with a silly Christmas apron on, a full feast before them, turkey, potatoes, sprouts, the works.

"When did you? How did you have time? Nick, you're the best!" She leaped forward, her arms encircling his neck before peppering his face with kisses.

"Sit down. Sit down," he said, prizing her off him as he pulled out a seat for her and handed her a cup of tea.

"Everything is ready, so feel free to begin whenever you want."

Lillian's mouth watered. Christmas dinner was always her favourite thing when she was younger, when her mother cooked it for them. The turkey looked wonderful, succulent and juicy, the mashed potatoes creamy and the sprouts with a little crunch and tiny pieces of bacon through them.

She piled her plate high, excited that the magic of Christmas was once again feeling like part of her life.

She pushed her plate away from her, after she had finished everything on the plate. "You are too good to me," she said, wiping her hands on the napkin.

"Well," Nick started shuffling his chair closer to her. "I have one more surprise for you." He handed her a beautifully wrapped box. It had white paper with glittery snowflakes on it and a black ribbon wrapped in a perfect little bow on top.

She smiled as he handed her the gift. "Thank you," she said, as she delicately opened the bow and removed the lid. "You really didn't have to. Dinner was more than enough."

She gasped as she looked at the intricate piece of jewellery inside. It was a silver necklace, with a small heart, inside the small heart sat a little robin which fluttered and flew around the heart.

"A magical piece?" she asked, tracing the robin with her finger. It chirped back at her before nuzzling her finger and then flying on again.

"Well, whilst you were studying with Julius, I may have looked into how to make this for you," he nervously said, playing with the hem of the tablecloth before him. "I really hope you like it. I know how much robins mean to you."

"You made it?" she said, shock evident in her voice. "You are amazing."

"You deserve the best," Nick replied, smiling his usual happy grin at her.

She stood up from her chair, and moved across to where Nick was sitting. She gently placed herself on his lap, cradling his face with her hands as she bent down and kissed him. It wasn't passionate or frenzied but a sweet kiss that showed him every ounce of what she felt about him.

She drew back, meeting his gaze with warmth, hoping he could see in her eyes how much this moment meant to her. She had never spent Christmas with a loved one before, normally she spent it by herself, and despite how the day had started, she was content.

He picked up the necklace and placed it around her neck, moving her hair out of the way to clasp it for her.

They walked through to the living room and sat down on the sofa, ready to watch a classic Christmas film, whatever was on the TV. She looked out the window and smiled to herself.

"It's snowing," she squealed excitedly.

Nick stood up, helping her in the process too. "Well, let's go play," he said, dragging her to the door, where he helped her shrug her coat on before putting his on. They put on their winter boots, hats and scarves before running out the door. Nick was in his element, he loved the snow and smiled as he looked up to the sky, embracing the beauty and magic that it brought.

He was brought out of his reverie when a giant snowball hit him in the back. Lillian giggled as she ducked behind a tree. A full-blown snowball fight broke out, which ended with Nick on the snowy ground and Lillian on top of him, kissing like a bunch of teenagers. To Lillian, it was perfect.

They headed inside once the sky got dark, changing into new pyjamas that they had both received from Nick's parents, part of a tradition that Nick's family had done for as long as he could remember, and sat in front of the TV with large cups of hot chocolate. Lillian looked up and patted Nick's thigh.

"Look, she's back," she said, pointing to the window. Sure enough, sitting on the window ledge, chirping away, was a little robin, with a bright red chest. She had a twig of Holly with some berries in her mouth, which it dropped when it saw Lillian approach. She opened the window and picked it up, twiddling the stem around in her fingers.

"Merry Christmas to you too, little friend," she said before closing the window and curtains and going back to the warmth of Nick.

"What's wrong?" he enquired as the film was coming to an end, lazily rubbing circles onto her back as she cuddled into his side.

"Nothing," she sighed happily. "Just thinking how we have made today the best day ever…"

Nick smiled at her, the happiest he had ever felt, grateful for the fact he had started his channel, used that catchphrase and now had her in life. Best Christmas ever.

Chapter Twenty-Two

Nick stood with Lillian in his mother and father's living room, a glass of champagne in their hand.

"Are you ready for another crazy year together?" he said above the music. Lillian giggled and nodded her head.

"Always ready to spend time with you," she replied, clinking her glass against his.

They turned to each other as the countdown timer started to go off, everyone else in the room blurring into the background, only eyes for each other.

Ten, nine, eight, seven, six, five, four, three, two, one!

"Happy new year!" they both exclaimed at the same time before coming together in an affectionate kiss. Nick cupped her jaw with one hand whilst the other threaded through her hair.

As they separated, they looked at each other, alone in their own little bubble. A throat cleared to the left of them as Nick pulled Lillian closer, his arms enclosed around her waist.

Lillian turned round in Nick's arms, looking at the culprit who had just interrupted them.

"Scarlet, what are you doing here?" Lillian stated, shocked at her colleagues' appearance.

Scarlet smiled, her perfectly painted lips curling upwards. "Did Nicky here not tell you that my father is friends with his?"

Nick looked at her, his eyes narrowing in at Scarlet. Lillian looked between the two of them, a confused look on her face.

"Nick?" Lillian inquired.

Nick snarled. "I told you not to call me Nicky." He turned to Lillian and looked at her helplessly. "I'll tell you soon," he whispered into her ear, making her shiver.

"Anyway," Scarlet said, rolling her eyes. "I just thought I'd give you these. A way of us putting the past behind us." She handed a flute of champagne to Lillian and one to Nick. Lillian smiled as she took the glass as did Nick. He stayed close to her as they all clinked glasses in a toast to the New Year.

They each downed their glass before Scarlet sauntered away, sending a flirty wink over her shoulder at Nick.

Nick rolled his eyes as he took Lillian's hand and led her to the balcony.

They closed the door behind them and Nick wrapped his arms around Lillian's waist and pulled her close, burying his face in her hair.

"My father and her father tried to set us up, some kind of business deal. I wasn't interested, never have been, but she didn't give up so easy. We went on one date and nothing more, I promise," he said, placing a kiss on her cheek.

"Okay," she whispered, laying her head on his shoulder.

The snow started to fall as they stood on the balcony. They watched as the blanket fell over everything in sight. Lillian started to shiver, so Nick guided her inside.

"I'm just going to go get us some drinks," he said, kissing her knuckles as he slowly backed away from her.

She giggled as she moved to sit down on an empty chair. Her head started to feel fuzzy, she couldn't see straight in front of her. The last thing she saw before she blacked out was a perfectly painted pair of red lips.

Lillian woke up in pure darkness, the sound of music banging around her. She felt her way to a standing position, fabric making her feel like she was suffocating.

She found the door in front of her and pulled the handle open. The party was still in full swing. She looked around for a clock, her vision still a little blurry, and noticed it was two a.m. She had been out for just under two hours.

She looked around and saw Victoria, a glass of champagne in her elegantly manicured fingers.

"Have you seen Nick?" she asked, slurring her words slightly.

"Oh my dear, I think you've had enough," Victoria said, laughing slightly. "He was beside the buffet the last I saw him." She pointed in the direction of the food and turned back to her conversation.

She walked through to find Nick and instantly saw him. He had his back turned to her and then she saw who he was talking to. Scarlet. Scarlet smirked as she made eye contact with Lillian, before she wrapped her fingers around the back of his neck and pulled him in for a passionate kiss.

Lillian stood watching the scene before her unfold. She turned to leave, her anger rising, magic fizzing from her every pore. She changed her mind and stormed over to the couple. She pulled Scarlet off Nick and slapped her square across the cheek, before turning to Nick and doing the exact same thing to him.

She turned on her heel and left the room with an explosion of magic in her wake, tears streaming down her face.

"Lillian, wait!" Nick shouted as he came running down the path after her.

"What Nick? What excuse do you have for her lips being on yours? For me being passed out in a cupboard for two hours and you not coming to find me…" she said angrily, turning to stare him in the eyes.

"I didn't know… I'm so sorry. It's no excuse really… I didn't kiss her, she kissed me. It's not an excuse but if you'd stayed around a little longer you would have seen me push her away, but you got there before me…" he said, rambling his explanation.

"Who said chivalry was dead?" she responded callously.

He snorted and threw his hands in the air. "What do you want me to do? I didn't want to kiss her. The only person I ever want to kiss again, for the rest of my life, is you…"

She looked at him and saw the sincerity in his eyes.

"Fuck it," she mumbled before she placed her hands on his shoulders, pulling his mouth to hers in a searing kiss.

Her hands left his shoulders and moved upwards until her fingers knotted in his raven-black hair. She twisted and pulled, roughly beckoning him closer, and he happily complied. Their lips met with more force, and she couldn't help thinking how glorious it was. When his hand then all of a sudden squeezed her thigh, Lillian could not stifle an unintentional whimper. The increased physical contact felt marvellous, though their positioning, with their legs trapped between their entwined bodies, did make things a bit difficult. Still, wanting more, Lillian leaned forward and pressed herself against him as much as she possibly could. In return, Nick let out a deep rumbling sound. She sensed him tighten his grip around her thigh and squealed into his mouth when he suddenly lifted her up and pulled her towards him, seemingly without any effort. She soon found herself on top of him, straddling his lap.

He pulled away slowly, a soft smile gracing his features.

"I have a confession to make," Lillian started. "I like the way you touch me."

She reached out and took his face into her quivering hands.

"I like the way you kiss me." She pressed a soft, closed-mouthed peck onto his unmoving lips.

"I-I," she stammered, her voice but a whisper. "I like the way you make me feel. You make me feel alive."

He could smell the champagne on her breath and knew they had both had far too much to drink, but couldn't help the fact he wanted her close.

In an instant, his lips were back on hers. His insistent tongue delved into her mouth, ravishing her mercilessly, and Lillian could not help but mewl when his hands moved downwards and took a firm hold of her rear. His touch felt divine, and it made her body ache in all the good ways.

"I need to be good and stop this. Be good for both of us. I think that we both go to sleep now, and in the morning, sober, having talked this through, start the New Year in the best way possible." He winked at her as he picked her up, slowly unzipping her dress. "Bed!"

The frigid air hit her bare skin like an arctic breeze and made every single hair on her body rise into goosebumps. Lillian shivered, though she was not quite sure whether that was by virtue of the cold or rather the way his calloused hands felt against her back. They roamed her body, travelling from her waist, up her spine all the way to her shoulder blades, caressing her as Nick kissed her again, softly and sweetly this time.

He ran up the stairs with her giggling in his arms as they snuggled up in bed, ready to start the New Year together, all the stronger for what they had just been through.

Chapter Twenty-Three

Lillian stood with her back pressed against the hard, cool wall. She breathed slow and hard, trying to catch her breath as Nick appeared beside her.

"Hey," he said, pecking her cheek.

"Hey yourself," she said as she looked around the corner, giving him a big smile. "How's your day going?"

Nick laughed, "Oh, you know, being chased by an angry seven-foot warlock, who doesn't want my father to take him. The joys…"

Lillian put her hand on his wrist and rubbed small circles where her initials were. "See you for dinner tonight?"

Nick nodded his head and Lillian reached up on her tiptoes, kissing his cheek before dashing off to carry on the job. Nick watched her retreating form and smirked, proud of the fact that this was his girl.

Lillian ran ahead, swerving past bushes and trees, trying to avoid running into any obstacles in her way. Her senses told her exactly where she needed to be and unfortunately, she knew this area well. The wind blew around her and she embraced the cold.

She walked down the familiar gravel path taking a turn to her right, slowing down to try and catch her breath.

She could hear a branch snapping in the distance and stood still. She took a deep breath before taking a running start in the direction of the noise.

She saw a being about five-foot-six, not much taller than herself, hunched over in front of her.

"You can't take me. I'm too young to go," the voice of a young woman said, looking up from her spot on the ground.

Lillian gasped as she looked at the young girl in front of her. She had been attacked and beaten. She was covered in blood and was protecting something on the ground.

"It's not you I'm here for…" was all Lillian said, before a tear streaked down her face. She quickly wiped it away. The woman before her sobbed, her dark hair hanging around her face like a blanket.

"Do you need me to get you some help before I go?"

The girl shook her head as she stretched her arms out, handing Lillian a tiny little baby.

"Please make sure he goes to a good place. He's too young. I tried to protect him." The girl sobbed. Lillian nodded her head as she wrapped the little bundle up.

"I will do what I can," she said, cradling him in her arms.

With that she turned and walked away from the crying mother. She walked further than normal. Usually, she would use her magic to get her and the client back to Steve, but she needed to make sure that the girl got help.

She walked to the town, gently cooing at the baby, who had fallen asleep, his tiny little hands grasping at the fabric wrapped around him.

177

"Excuse me, I was wondering if you could help. I need to get the baby back into the warmth but I think I saw a girl who has been hurt running towards the graveyard. Is there any chance you could go check?" she asked a group of gentlemen who were walking past.

One nodded his head and they rushed off in the direction that Lillian had just come from. As soon as they were out of sight, Lillian vanished from sight, leaving a dark shadow in her wake.

She appeared in Steve's office, who was sitting with Nick, the baby still in her arms.

"Lillian, what are you doing here?" Steve asked, "Are you not on a mission tonight?"

Lillian shushed the little bundle in her arms and thrust him into Nick's arms.

"Yes! Yes, I was. I am not okay with this," she shouted pointing at the cooing baby in Nick's arms. "The baby is fine, healthy and you made me take him from his mother! I can't… I left her beaten and crying and she was like me… She was the same height, the same build, the same age and I had to take her baby from her."

She collapsed into the chair, holding her head in her hands and openly crying in front of everyone.

The baby responded to Lillian's wails and started to cry as well.

"Take the baby out of here Nick. Take him to the office while I speak to Lillian. He needs to move on."

Nick looked at Lillian and then at his father, before nodding his head. He walked to Lillian, before kissing the crown of her head and then disappeared from sight with the little bundle in tow.

"Lillian, you can't get emotional, it isn't that sort of job," Steve started.

"No!" she interrupted him. "I didn't want this job. You cannot blame me for getting emotional when I have to take a baby from his mother to take him to the afterlife. All I kept thinking was how I would feel if this was happening to me…"

Steve sighed. "You are just like your mother. Empathetic. It is a great quality to have, but can get you into a lot of danger." Steve walked over to his desk and pulled out a file. He flicked through the pages, before finding the information about the baby.

"Jack was ill. He had been from the moment he was born. His mother had used magical hormones whilst she was pregnant which caused issues that the naked eye couldn't see. It caused his cells to be overrun with magic that was essentially trying to kill him from the moment of his birth. You helped him and did a good thing. I'm not always the bad guy, we aren't always the bad guys in this situation. Jack can now be at peace. He can move on." Steve patted Lillian on the back as he handed her the file for Jack and walked back to his seat, letting her read the information in front of her. She stood up from her seat, walking toward the window to read the information in Jack's file. She took a seat on the floor and looked up, taking a big sigh. As she looked out the window, a little robin appeared, tilting her head at Lillian. Their eyes connected and Lillian swore that she saw them sparkle.

"The father's the one that beat her up, wasn't he? He was the one that hurt her. He found out that she was using these hormones, trying to make little Jack something that he wasn't. He wasn't magical at all, apart from what these hormones gave him. That's why we had to take him, isn't it?"

Steve slowly nodded his head.

Lillian shook slightly. "I apologise for bursting in here like that. I am going to go home now. Thank you, Mr Madden," she said before getting up from her spot on the floor and handing him the file back. "Is there a way that I can find out about Jack in the future?"

Steve nodded. "I'll see what I can do for you. Now go home, relax."

Lillian turned to leave before Steve spoke again, "Oh and Lillian, good job tonight. I know that wasn't easy."

She smiled at him before disappearing from sight.

She appeared in Nick's house and crumbled into a heap on the floor.

"I can't take this anymore," she cried out to the empty room.

Just the thought of that tiny, little baby brought a fresh wave of tears to her eyes. Eventually she couldn't cry any more. There was nothing left. She was exhausted, but couldn't even consider sleeping.

A noise was made to her right, but she was too exhausted to move and the next thing she knew, she was being picked up and carried into a bedroom.

"Sssh," Nick whispered, as he gently stroked her hair, moving it out of her face. "I'm going to take care of you now."

Slowly, he slipped her dirty clothes from her, crumpling them up and putting them into the washing basket at the other side of the room, before picking her up again and moving her to the bath. He had already filled it up with water and bubbles and lovely scents that filled her foggy brain. Next, he took a washcloth and slowly washed every inch of her, careful not to put too much pressure on any cuts and bruises, but all the time, whispering reassurances in her ear.

When she was clean and her hair had been washed and gently brushed, Nick wrapped a towel around her and helped her out of the bath. He escorted her to the bedroom and helped to dry and dress her in her comfiest pyjamas before turning the bed cover over and helping her underneath them, into the warmth.

He walked around and got in the other side. "Sssh. I'm here now, I have you," he said, gathering her in close.

Chapter Twenty-Four

Nick sat across from Lillian, who was once again curled up on the beanbag in his studio with a book open in her lap. One of her favourite places to be.

"I'm not going to lie. I'm a little nervous," Nick said, turning to face her. "It's been so long since I did this."

Lillian smiled warmly at him. "It could be years and you would still have their support. And you always have mine," she said, blowing a kiss in his direction.

He pretended to catch it and put it in his pocket for later, making her giggle.

He picked up his guitar, balancing it in his lap as he took a deep breath, before pressing the button to start the live stream.

Three, two, one. "Hello strangers," he said, getting into the swing of things straight away and Lillian couldn't help the grin that appeared on her face. He was in his element, in his happy place.

Lillian curled up tighter under the blanket and drifted to sleep as Nick started chatting away, lulling her into slumber.

She awoke to find Nick's beaming face hovering above her.

"Hello sleepy head," he said, leaning down to give her a sweet kiss. "We're going for an adventure today, if you're up for it."

Lillian smiled at him happily.

"You mean more of an adventure than what we do for a living?" she asked, raising her eyebrow in his direction.

Nick wrapped his arm around Lillian as he whisked her out of the room in a swoosh of magic.

They landed on a dusky little path, hidden by some tall cascading trees. He took her hand in his and gently guided her out into the open sunshine. He wrapped a scarf around her neck to protect her from the chill of the air.

He ushered her over to a bench and they both took a seat, Nick taking a deep breath of fresh air.

Lillian looked out over the pond in front of her, little ducks happily swimming away, kids squealing as they played in the park opposite them. The wind swirled round them, picking up leaves and making them dance before her very eyes.

Nick looked at ease as Lillian observed him. "Where are we?" she asked, smiling gently at him.

"I know, it's not very exciting, but this was my favourite place to come when I was growing up. It was always so peaceful and mother and I would often come here just to escape for a few hours," he explained.

He pointed over to the left of the pond. "That was where I first learned to ride my bike. Over there was where I broke my arm from skateboarding. And this spot it where I first fell in love with the guitar. There was an old man.

He would sit here and play his guitar and every time we would come and see him play, he would hand me some bread for the ducks. It was my favourite place in the entire world."

Lillian smiled fondly at Nick. "Thank you for sharing this place with me," she whispered, leaning over to press a kiss on his cheek.

"Let's go for a walk," Nick said, standing up suddenly. He held his hand out for Lillian who happily took it. They wandered around the outside of the pon, when Nick saw a little girl with her dad.

"But Daddy. I want to feed the ducks!" she cried out, tears streaming her face. Lillian looked over at Nick who smiled at her, before moving his hands in a figure of eight motion. A bag of bread appeared in his hand and he slowly walked over to the family.

"Sorry to intrude," he started as he got closer, "I couldn't help but overhear, but I have some spare bread if you would like it."

Her eyes lit up and she looked at her dad with pleading eyes. He nodded his head mouthing, "Thank you," to Nick who just smiled happily back.

The little girl came running up to him and wrapped her tiny arms around his waist, giving him a squeeze. He looked over at Lillian who beamed at him as he hugged her back. "Thank you!" she exclaimed, running over to feed the duckling that was not far from her.

Lillian hugged Nick tightly. "That was adorable," she said, smiling brightly as they walked away from the pond. "Thank you for sharing somewhere so special with me."

"Anytime. Hopefully someday we can take our kids here," he said, squeezing her tight, She smiled slightly, her heartrate increasing at the thought of a little baby with Nick's green eyes and curly hair.

Chapter Twenty-Five

They were out on the job and Lillian had just finished taking a six-foot odd monster to Steve, and was waiting for Nick when she felt a shooting pain go through her. She screamed out in pain as she fell to the ground. Victoria came running to her side, kneeling down beside her.

"What's wrong my dear?" she asked, wrapping an arm around her shoulder.

Lillian started to sob, just as Steve approached them. "Nick…" She cried, clutching her chest.

"The twin flame," Victoria said, looking up at her husband. Victoria reached over to Lillian and pushed her hair behind her ear. The mark was slowly fading.

"No!" Victoria stated, tears filling her eyes.

Lillian stood up quickly and disappeared out the room in a flash of red. Her partner was hurt, she knew it deep down. She was upset but she was angry. How dare someone hurt her Nick!

She appeared in an alleyway in the middle of town. The wind whipped around her, chilling her to the bone. She had forgotten to put her coat on before she left the house to find Nick and was now feeling it.

Suddenly, warmth overwhelmed her and she looked at her feet to see a little fireball of magic floating at her feet. *Neat,* she thought to herself.

A feeling of dread overtook her suddenly as the pain within her chest continued. She took off and quickly as she could until she reached a dead-end. She panted with exertion, jumping over a broken tree branch as she sprinted across the street and finally slowed down, pausing to stretch her pleasantly sore muscles and catch her breath.

She heard a groan of pain nearby and her blood turned cold. She ran over to where the bins were and behind them was Nick, slouched over, bleeding badly from cuts in his chest, leg and a gash on his neck.

She bent down beside him, ripping her shirt to put over the wound on his neck applying pressure.

"Don't you dare! Nicholas Madden, you cannot leave me. You are my soulmate. We are going to get married and have a family and grow old together. You cannot die on me!" she shouted. She placed one hand on his chest and started to feel his heart weaken and struggle. Her hand balled up into a fist and she struck him firmly across the chest with a grunt of effort and anger. It was instinct, something she remembered from first aid training or maybe from a TV show she had once watched, she thought. But she couldn't care less where she'd learnt it from as long as it worked. And work it did, as his heart stuttered only for half a second before picking back up much steadier now that it was forced into action.

"That's it, and don't you dare do that again," she warned, rubbing away the moisture falling down her cheeks. With a sudden incantation that suddenly popped into her head from recent reading, the wound on his neck closed up but there was a lot of work that needed to go into stabilising him properly and getting him home was the first step in that.

She crouched down beside him, grabbing his hand, focusing hard on where she wanted to go and muttered 'Adventure achieved' before they disappeared from the dark, dingy alleyway.

With a pop, they appeared in Nick's parents living room.

"Help!" Lillian shouted, placing Nick on the sofa, not caring about the blood stains that she was getting everywhere.

"What happened?" Steve asked, approaching as his wife appeared behind him and screamed, running over to her son and stroking his head.

"I did the best I could out there, but needed to get him somewhere safe to look at his wounds better." She refused to leave Nick's side. She was determined to help as much as she could.

Victoria openly sobbed looking at her son's motionless body as Steve fussed over the wounds on his legs. Lillian took his shirt and ripped it open, exposing the wounds on his chest. She focused all her magic on the wound and trained it to the area it needed to go. "Save him," she muttered to herself. "Please save him."

Victoria cried out. "Lillian, your mark. It's gone dark again!" She started to openly sob again. Steve moved away from his son, wiping the blood off his hands before turning to Lillian.

"Good job, my dear. Thank you for helping save Nick," Steve said, patting her on the shoulder as he left the room.

Victoria threw herself at Lillian and hugged her tightly. "You saved him! Thank you. Thank you." She kissed Lillian's cheek as she hugged her tightly.

Lillian sighed, the adrenaline of the situation fading from her system. She crumbled into a heap in Victoria's arms and started to sob.

Victoria helped her to her feet as they left Nick to wake up on the sofa. "Come on, I'll give you something to change into. You ruined your shirt trying to save my son's life. I owe you so much."

Victoria escorted Lillian out of the room and into one of the many bathrooms in their house.

"You bathe and I'll lay out something for you to wear. I'll let you know as soon as Nick wakes up." Victoria smiled at Lillian and squeezed her hand gently before turning to leave the room.

Lillian turned on the faucet and let the water heat up as she looked at herself in the mirror. Her hair was stained red as was her ripped t-shirt, her eyes were puffy and swollen and she looked like she needed to sleep for at least a week. She had saved him though. It was all worth it.

She stripped off her torn clothes and climbed into the shower, letting the hot water cascade over her sore and achy body. She tried not to think about Nick and the state he was in or what would have happened if she hadn't got to him in time. Instead, she scrubbed at her hair and then her body, trying to get the blood off her skin.

Once the water started to run clear, she stepped out of the stream and wrapped a towel around her body and one around her hair. She walked across the large room to where Victoria had left some clothes for her. She picked up the dress and sighed, it was not her normal taste, but she was grateful anyway.

She disposed of the towels and slid into the clothes provided for her. She ran her hand through her hair, trying to brush out the tangles and pushed it out of her eye. She took a long look at herself in the full-length mirror and for once was confident in the way she looked. She felt pretty and desirable; Nick's mum had an amazing choice in clothing. She thought to herself about asking Victoria about going on a shopping spree some time as she could use the help and it would also be great to get to know her more without the men in the family being there.

There was a knock on the bathroom door, interrupting Lillian's thoughts.

"Come in," she said, turning to face the door.

Victoria burst through the door. "My dear, you look beautiful," she said looking Lillian over before remembering her reason for coming in. "Nick's awake. He's asking for you."

Lillian rushed towards Victoria, linking their arms in the process as the ran out of the room, towards Nick.

Nick was laying on the sofa, an arm resting behind his head as his mother walked into the room, happy tears running down her face.

"She's just coming dear," she said, pressing a kiss to her son's cheek.

Lillian walked into the room and smiled at Nick as she rushed to his side.

"I'm so happy you are okay. I've never been so scared in my life," she cried, as she crouched down beside him.

"Lillian, you look stunning!" Nick said, with a croaky voice, turning to face her completely.

Lillian blushed. "All thanks to your mother, I'm afraid. Are you okay?" She brushed her hand gently across his cheek.

"I'm a little sore," he replied, his voice low and rasping.

Lillian laughed before punching him in the arm. "Don't you ever do that to me again!" she said angrily, "I cannot lose you!"

Nick winced at her punch but laughed at her reaction. He placed his hands, one on either side of her face and pulled her lips to his in a romantic kiss.

"I promise, I will never let that happen again," he said sincerely.

"Good," was all she responded before launching herself at him and smothering him in kisses.

Chapter Twenty-Six

He ran a hand down her back, gently rubbing circles as he went.

"So, on a scale of one to ten, how bad an idea do you think it would be if we got married?"

"Off the scale..." A smirk appeared on her face. "Let's do it."

"So..."

"So, we're engaged?" she asked, her eyes twinkling, excitedly.

"Seems like it," he responded, smirking at the love of his life.

"This is going to piss a lot of people off," she replied. "Including your father."

He placed a hand in his trouser pocket and produced a little black box. Slowly, his fingers wrapped around it and opened to reveal a beautiful silver ring. He picked up her hand in his and gently slid the ring onto her finger.

"You just happen to carry this about with you?" she asked, admiring the beautiful piece of jewellery that now adorned her finger.

"Well, when your family is as old as mine is, you pick up a few heirlooms along the way." She held her hand up and looked at the ruby-red diamond, glittering in the dull light.

"Do I even want to know where you got it or from who?"

"I mean, you could just say thank you and tell me you love it," he smiled. "Your dad said you would like it. If you don't, we can get you something else."

Lillian's hands shot up to her mouth. "You saw my dad?"

He grabbed her hand and placed a kiss on her knuckles. "Of course. I am old-fashioned in some ways. I needed to ask his permission first. Not that he made it easy for me."

"He was sober?" she asked, watching as Nick nodded his head.

She threw her arms around his neck, jumping up and peppering kisses all over his face. "Thank you. Thank you. Thank you," she cried.

He laughed as she wrapped her legs around his waist. "Am I forgiven now?" he whispered into her ear before moving to kiss her neck.

"I suppose," she said through a moan.

"As much as I'd love to continue this, you need a shower, I need to change clothes as I'm now covered in blood and we have less than an hour until we have to meet them."

"Are you going to tell them?" she asked, still kissing his neck.

"Mmmm, you're going to have to stop that. I'm waiting to see how long it takes them to notice the ring. I reckon it'll be as soon as you get in the door. My mother loves you; you know? She's been asking since you walked in the door and I introduced you when I was going to propose." He gently placed her on the ground, kissing the crown of her head.

He held out his hand for her which she took and rubbed the ring as it lay on her finger. "Adventure achieved," he whispered before they were both whisked away in a blur of colour.

They appeared in his childhood bedroom, decorated with dark emerald-greens and gold. There were film posters on every wall as well as musical posters of his idols from when Nick was a child. He had vinyl's and CDs stacked everywhere along with books. It was similar to her own childhood room, just decorated in different colours.

They walked out hand in hand, towards the dining room, the light reflecting off the ring and catching Lillian's eye.

Nick pushed open the door and smiled at his mother. "Mother, father. Sorry to stop by unannounced. We were in the neighbourhood and I was wondering if it would be okay to show Lillian some of the books in the library. She is very interested in some of the natural forms of magic and I don't have any books on them in my flat," Nick said casually as he walked over and kissed his mother on the cheek.

"Is that all my dear?" she asked. "Nothing else to tell us, or show us?"

Lillian had to hand it to Victoria. She was very quick and paid special attention to detail. She got up out of her seat and was over to her in a second, pulling her hand up to admire the ring that now adorned Lillian's finger.

"Congratulations, my love. Welcome to the family," she said, kissing both her cheeks. "If it had been up to me, he would've done it months ago," she whispered in Lillian's ear.

Lillian blushed as she noticed Steve look up from his book, obviously curious as to what his wife was getting excited about. He muttered a 'congratulations' and left the room, his book tucked under his arm.

Lillian turned to Victoria who just shrugged. "Nick, you go find some books for the lovely Lillian. We have to have some girl chat and I don't want you to get bored. Now disappear." She indicated for him to leave and he did so, not before leaving a kiss on her cheek and Lillian's.

"Now, I know it is soon, but we must start planning. Big or small wedding? Indoor or outdoor? White or ivory dress? What sort of flowers? I'm sorry I'm just excited. I never thought I would get this opportunity. Nick never seemed like the sort who would want to get married and now here he is," Victoria squealed, holding onto Lillian's hand and dancing round in a circle.

Lillian couldn't help the laugh that escaped as the two of them danced around the dining room like a pair of children.

"Thank you so much," Lillian said as they sat back down and Victoria poured them both a cup of tea. "It's nice to have someone to help me with all of this. Especially since Mum isn't here any more," she said sniffling.

Victoria put her tea down and moved to the seat beside Lillian. She pulled her in close and hugged her tightly. "I will always be here for you. If you need anything, just let me know. You will soon be my daughter-in-law and I cannot wait for you to be a part of this family." Lillian smiled and hugged Victoria back.

"What have I missed?" Nick said with a grin on his face as he walked in with a stack of books. "I leave you alone for ten minutes and you have my future bride in tears. Mother…"

"Just girl chat, my love," she said, warning him not to push it.

"I love you Mum," Nick said, placing a gentle kiss on her cheek. She smiled at her son and got up to give him an embrace.

"Thank you for giving me such a lovely daughter-in-law," she said before returning to her own seat.

Nick smiled down at Lillian. "Would you like to take a walk through the gardens before we go home? You could maybe see some flowers you like for the wedding. I'm sure mother would love that." He held out his arm like a gentleman for her and she graciously accepted, waving a small goodbye to Victoria before exiting the room.

They walked in silence as they headed out to the gardens. "It's so beautiful out here and peaceful," Nick stated as they walked into the maze of flowers. "It's also where I wrote part of your song."

Lillian couldn't help but blush. "Why don't we get married here then? We wouldn't need to get any flowers, everything is all so beautiful as it is, and we can show off all the wonderful work that your mother put into these gardens over the years. It would be perfect," she stated, spinning round on the spot, admiring the view around her.

"Agreed," Nick said, walking over and picking her up. "I can't wait to marry you here. Now let's get home. I believe we started something earlier; I would love to continue."

Chapter Twenty-Seven

Ruby bounced into the room as Lillian napped on the sofa. "Lils, wake up," she gleefully shouted.

Lillian sat up, rubbing her eyes sleepily.

"Morning to you too," she muttered, making room for Ruby to sit down beside her. "Not that I don't want to see you, but why are you here?" she asked.

"First, to make you coffee. You are so grumpy first thing in the morning, and secondly, Tristan asked me to meet him here." Ruby walked through to the kitchen and put the kettle on.

"Okay, okay. I wouldn't be as grumpy if it wasn't for the fact that I got home at stupid o'clock of the morning. This job is worse than constant night shifts," Lillian said, combing a hand through her hair and tying it up in a bobble on top of her head.

"I know, but you kick ass at it," Ruby shouted through from the kitchen. "I've seen your records. You are beating the boys, hands down, with the work that you've been doing."

"Somehow, that doesn't make me feel better," Lillian muttered, wrapping a blanket around herself as she snuggled into the sofa.

There was a knock at the door and Ruby ran over to get it, handing Lillian a coffee on the way past.

"For you," she said, running to the door and throwing it open.

"Tristan, hi! Oh my God, Nick are you okay?" Ruby squealed.

Lillian shot up out of her seat, her coffee forgotten about and ran to the door. Tristan was standing in the doorway, supporting Nick's weight as he couldn't stand by himself.

"What happened?" she enquired.

"Let me get him to bed, then I'll come speak to you," he said, pecking Ruby on the cheek on the way past.

Lillian threw herself back onto the sofa, her eyebrows knotting together in worry and confusion.

"Stop freaking yourself out," Ruby said, sitting next to Lillian and taking her hand.

Tristan came back down the stairs and sat in the armchair, running his hand through his hair and sighing.

"Lils, have you noticed anything wrong with Nick recently?" he asked as Ruby went to make him a coffee as well.

Lillian sat up and thought about it. "Not that I'm aware of. He's been out working a lot. I get home and he's not always here and then he's not always here the next morning when I wake up either. I just thought he was getting the tough tasks. Like his father was testing him or something," she rambled on.

Tristan took the cup from Ruby and smiled softly at her.

"Thank you." He took a long sip before placing it down on the coffee table and reaching forward and grasping Lillian's hand.

"I'm going to tell you something and you aren't to blame yourself. It would be 100 times worse if it weren't for you. I think Nick has a problem…" he started explaining. "Do you have a liquor cabinet or anywhere you store alcohol?"

Lillian stood up and walked through to the kitchen and opened up the cupboard that the spirits were normally kept in. She sighed as she opened the door and the bottles inside were all empty.

"Oh Nick…" she sighed, shaking her head.

Tristan came over with Ruby not far behind. "Lils, we're here if you need help," she started.

Lillian turned round. "It's okay. Thank you for coming. I know you're worried about him. I am too, but you guys head home. I'm going to sober him up and we're going to have a big conversation," she said, a smile gracing her face that didn't quite reach her eyes.

She walked Ruby and Tristan to the door. "If you need anything, just call. I'm here for you, we both are. He's like a brother to me and if we need to, we'll all go cold turkey. If there's none here, he'll be less tempted," Tristan said, wrapping her in a friendly embrace.

"Thank you. Unfortunately, I have been here before. If he wants it, he will always find a way to get it. It'll be a hard conversation, but it needs to be had," Lillian said, tears threatening to spill from her eyes.

After she closed the door behind them, she walked to the kitchen and splashed some cool water on her face, trying to steady her nerves before heading upstairs. She grabbed a hangover cure from the little cafe that they often visited on the way out.

Nick was laying on the bed groaning. She propped him up and tilted his head back.

"Take this," she whispered, stroking his cheek. "You'll be fine in a few minutes."

She watched as the cure started to work. He looked at her with bloodshot eyes, full of worry.

"I went too far," he muttered, refusing to break eye contact.

She nodded her head, sadly, looking down at her hands.

"It won't happen again, I promised it was a one-time thing," he said, grabbing her hands and bringing them up to her lips.

"That's what he used to say... Every single damn time I came home and he was passed out drunk. It won't happen again Lilipad, I'm sorry. I've heard it all before..." Lillian crossed her legs in front of her on the bed, still refusing to look at him.

"I mean it. You are the most important thing to me Lillian. I will do anything to stop you from hurting. I can feel it in my chest. I can feel you hurting and I'm the one who has caused it. I don't want to be the one hurting you. Help me, please?" he begged, lying his head on her lap, his eyes pleading with hers.

Lillian had sworn to herself that she would be strong, but she could see the regret on his face. She sighed out loud.

"Okay," she said, threading her fingers through his curly hair. "No more alcohol!"

He nodded his head, closing his eyes as she gently scraped her nails along his scalp.

"I have one question though Nick," she spoke quietly as she continued to run her hands through his hair.

He hummed in an answer, his eyes closing in contentment. "Why?"

He looked up at her, tears threatening to spill from his vibrant green eyes. "I lost control. From when I was attacked. Everything spiralled. I can't keep you safe and I needed something…"

"To numb the pain," she finished, bending down and placing a brief kiss on his lips. "You know you can talk to me whenever you want or need to, no matter what the subject."

He nodded his head and pulled himself up onto his elbows to kiss her.

"Thank you," he muttered against her lips. "Thank you for saving me from myself."

Chapter Twenty-Eight

Nick had been sober for sixty days. They had cleared out all the cabinets, got rid of all the empty bottles and done a cleansing ritual to the house to rid of any bad omens.

During his recovery, Lillian made him speak to his mother and father and they had both agreed that whilst he was recovering, he would cut down the amount of work that he was doing and Lillian and Tristan would help pick up the work he was missing.

"I have a surprise for you tonight. To celebrate your sixty days sober," Lillian said, smiling brightly.

Nick spun her round in a circle under his arm, beaming at her. "You honestly don't have to do anything. Being able to spend time with you is more than enough," Nick responded, pulling her into his arms to dance with her.

"Oh, shush you. I want you to dress nicely tonight, maybe shirt and those jeans I love that make your butt look good," she said, slapping his bum as she walked away from him giggling. She looked back over her shoulder. "Oh and be ready for seven, please?" She winked and dashed up the stairs.

Nick laughed as he watched her retreating form. He was one lucky man.

Lillian walked down the stairs at seven, to see Nick standing there with a bunch of flowers, similar to the ones that he had bought her on their first date. She smiled as she approached and he handed her the bouquet, bending down to kiss her sweetly.

She looked stunning a blue velvet dress with a sweetheart neckline that cut off round her knees.

"You look phenomenal," he said, as she spun around on the spot.

"Thank you. You don't look too shabby yourself," she said, grabbing his hand and pulling him out of the door.

They walked outside and Nick opened the door of the car for Lillian before walking round to his side of the car. They drove in comfortable silence the majority of the way there. When they arrived at the little Italian restaurant, he gave her his elbow and helped her in and to their seat.

Lillian looked around the restaurant, the atmosphere quiet and exceedingly romantic with dim lights, red tablecloths, and chairs.

"I love you," he said like it was the first time he had said it to her out loud.

She stopped midway through her discussion of Ruby and Tristan's holiday plans and paused before she smiled at him.

"What was that for?" Her eyebrows arched, pretending that the words had not affected her, but the apparent blush on her face and the giggle that bubbled out of her mouth, still made it clear that Nick could still surprise her once in a while.

"No reason, just felt like saying it," he said simply, shrugging carelessly but at the same time, clearly amused by her blushing face.

They continued their conversation, both taking turns to decide the topic of conversation as they awaited their meal.

"I actually have something to show you later on," Lillian said, linking their hands together across the table. "I hope you like it as it's something very important to me."

They dined with light conversation as they twiddled spaghetti around their forks, continuing the discussion of their days and their plans for the upcoming wedding, Lillian and Victoria having already started to discuss details.

After dessert, the couple lapsed into comfortable and satiated silence. Nick called for the cheque and paid for it quickly.

"Are you ready?" he asked, offering his arm.

She nodded enthusiastically, her excitement and nervousness starting to show.

"Can I drive?" she asked, holding her hand out expectantly, waiting for the keys.

Nick laughed as he placed the keys to his car in her hands and she drove a little bit outside the town. She parked in a layby and dragged him by the hand into the middle of beautiful rock pools of crystal-clear spring water at the foot of the mountains that surrounded them.

"Are you ready for your surprise?" she asked, letting go of his hand. He nodded his head, excited to see what she was about to do. Her magic had gotten so much stronger recently and he was impressed every time he saw her perform anything.

She kicked off her shoes, placing them on a rock, before slowly wading into the water. With the setting sun came a sky of fire, the orange of every wintry hearth. It was the perfect time.

She bent down and ran her hands through the gently lapping water, look up, a smile gracing her lips. As she swirled her hands in the depths, something started to bubble the water, splashing around her as she stood up.

As she straightened up, the water started to rush up her legs, pushing her out of the pool and hoisting her up into the sky. The magic from the water and the earth dancing around Lillian as she stood in all her glory.

Nick stood on the spot. There was nothing he could do but watch the scene in front of him. He was mesmerised by the sight of the woman that he loved, the woman that he would soon marry, reaching the peak of her magic. It flowed out of her like streams of colourful ribbons, wrapping around her, entangling with her limbs, through her hair into the air and pushing outwards. He could feel it wash over him, a feeling that he was used to after all the time that they had spent practising together. His magic mixed with hers and he felt complete.

Lillian was lowered to the ground, curled up into a small ball. Nick ran over to her as she stood up tall. Her dress was a sheer black colour, showing off magical runes that now adorned her arms and legs, her hair, no longer the beautiful ivory colour it had been, but now mixed with the colours of her elemental magic.

She smiled the most radiant smile that Nick had ever seen come from her as she reached him. "Hello, my love," she said, wrapping her arms around his neck and pulling him in close for a sensual kiss.

"What was that for?" he asked, a smirk gracing his features.

"Well, if it hadn't been for you, I never would have been able to realise my full potential. I may have been upset to start with being put in the position that we were but now everything has worked out and I have something for you," she said, smiling brightly at him.

She waved her hands in front of them both in a figure of eight motion and conjured up a small box, handing it to Nick. He took it from her, grazing his hands across the inside of his wrist where his initials were and placing a kiss on her cheek. He slowly took the lid off the box and unwrapped its contents. Inside was a small t-shirt which said, 'Be Nice to Me. My Daddy Knows How to Dispose of a Dead Body'. Nick gasped and laughed in the same motion, dropping the shirt to the ground and wrapping Lillian up in a giant bear hug, spinning her round on the spot.

"My body reacted to our little devil. I can feel the magic rushing through me. It's the most powerful feeling that I have ever felt," she said, the feeling of happiness making her dizzy. "You're going to be a dad."

He peppered kisses all over her face and down her neck as she squealed with happiness.

"We need to find a way to tell my parents. My mother will be ecstatic. I reckon my father will be super happy too. And then the guys we stream with. They always want to know how you are doing and I want to make a video just for this. Oh, I know." Lillian leaned forward and pressed her lips firmly against Nick's.

"Honey, you're rambling," she said, taking his hands and placing them on her stomach. He couldn't stop smiling and placing random kisses all over her face. He slowly fell to his knees and wrapped his arms around her waist, placing a delicate kiss on her stomach.

"I love you little one. Dada's here." Lillian felt the tears spring to her eyes and wiped her eyes with the back of her hand. She was truly happy for the first time in her life and nothing would be able to spoil it.

Chapter Twenty-Nine

Things were good, better than good... for a while. Lillian was having meetings with Nick and his mother about the wedding. It was to be in the summer, not too many people there, immediate family only and her father was not to be invited, despite him trying to make amends with his daughter. They would have roses and sunflowers everywhere, to symbolise their first date and how far they had come together. It was going to be perfect.

Work wasn't too bad either. She was getting stronger, her magic, her ability to work alone or with Nick and Tristan, all was improving. She was now a vital part of the team. She was content.

One day she came home from shopping with Ruby. They had been going to try on bridesmaids' dresses and had some lunch, but she had been tired so asked if they could head home. The door was open, just a crack. Lillian pushed it open, a hand over Ruby protectively as she slid into the door.

"Lillian, is that you?" she heard Tristan shout from another room. She ran forward, forgetting about Ruby, her bags and everything else.

"Tristan, what's up?" she asked as she bolted into the bathroom.

Tristan stood, his arms folded over his broad chest, tapping his foot. "I'm sorry. I found him like this. If you need any help, let me know," he said, leaving her alone in the bathroom with Nick laid in the bathtub.

"What the hell Nick?" she shouted, slapping him on the shoulder, anger fizzing within her, making her magic erupt from her.

"Woah," was the only response she got from him as he watched the colours swirl around her.

He leaned forward and placed his hands on her belly. "Daddy messed up, sorry little one. Please forgive me. I want to be better for you. I just don't know how…" And then he passed out again.

"Oh, for Christ's sake," Lillian muttered as she wordlessly cast a levitation spell and carried him out of the bathroom and dropped him on the bed. She rolled him on his side and grabbed a basin to put beside the bed. She slowly walked downstairs, her hand caressing her stomach as she went to get him a glass of water. She filled the glass and headed back upstairs and put it on the bedside table, before bending and placing a soft kiss on his forehead, brushing his hair out of the way.

"Oh Nick, what am I going to do with you?" she asked, stroking his cheek.

She padded downstairs and walked to the kitchen she opened every cupboard and took everything out of them searching for any alcohol that she had missed. She knew it was pointless. She had lived with her father and dealt with it there too. If an alcoholic wanted a drink, there was no way to stop them. It would only work if he wanted to stop himself. She sat down on the kitchen chair, suddenly exhausted and started to sob. Everything had become too much. She needed to go home. She smiled sadly as she looked around Nick's house.

She grabbed a bit of paper and left him a note before disappearing out of sight.

Dear Nick, the love of my life,

My heart is breaking as I write this. I am going home for a little while. I need to clear my head. Get some space. When you are ready to talk and get sober, not for me, for this little one and for your own good, then come find me.

I will love you until the day that I die.

Lils x

Chapter Thirty

It was six excruciating long days before he found her. Six days for her to think and get more pissed off.

"You are the lightning and I am the thunder. We bring destruction with us everywhere. We are the villains. You've broken me and if I have to, I will destroy you," she said, looking him directly in the eye, towering over him as he sat in the seat, swirling the scotch around the glass in his hand.

"We had a job to do. You made it so much worse and left me! You left me. You left us! I'm not living this life any more… I'm surviving and I hate to break it to you but it was you that did that to me. You and only you!" She took the glass from him, poured the liquid onto the ground and threw the crystal into the fireplace across the room from them, watching the flames roar to life.

Nick looked up at her pacing the room. "Well, you know what they say," he said shrugging as he levitated a glass over to his now empty hand and filled it with more amber liquid. "It's better a broken heart, than a broken neck. Or losing this child because you've been selfish and not been careful."

The crack that resounded across the room as Lillian's hand connected with Nick's jaw was deafening.

"You absolute bastard! I thought I meant something to you," Lillian said, her voice cracking as the emotion that she'd been bottling up threatened to become exposed. Her blood ran cold as she saw the change in Nick's eyes.

"That's the problem isn't it. You overthink everything," he said, downing the glass and not breaking eye contact. She walked over to him and put her hand on the bottle and spoke quietly, 'Adventure achieved'.

Nick ran his hands through his hair. "Fuck!" he shouted into the empty room. She didn't associate the computer with him any more, but the bottle of whisky. He stood up and started moving round the room, kicking and punching everything in his path. He threw open the door and stormed down the hall to his father's office.

"We need to talk!" He slammed his fist down on the table making everything shake.

"Son," Steve said, looking up from his papers.

"Take her off the case! Take her off the damn case! I can't cope with this any more. I am literally drinking myself to your door to deal with Lillian working for you. I am killing myself and losing her at the same time. You need to protect her, make sure she is okay. She is my everything. Dad, please?" Nick begged as he openly sobbed in front of his father.

Steve got up and came round to his son. "I need you to sober up. You will never be able to do anything in this state. I will consider your wish, but look after yourself," he said, patting Nick on the shoulder before leaving the study.

"Nick, honey, are you okay?" a female voice said, approaching him. Mrs Miller placed her hand gently on his back, rubbing small circles.

"I need help!" Nick cried out, looking up into her kind eyes.

"I know honey. I know. Let me help you," she said, helping him up out of the seat, as his sobbing continued. His body was overcome with guilt. He had promised that he would love her, he was bound to her and his soul hurt. She'd been away for less than half an hour, but he was physically hurt from her absence.

"Okay, first thing's first, shower for you," she said, pushing him along the corridor to his room.

Mrs Miller took the clothes from him as he headed into the bathroom for his shower and took them to be washed, to get the stench of alcohol out of the fabric.

He emerged from the shower with warm, fluffy towels wrapped around him and perched on the end of the bed.

"I've messed this up, haven't I? I promised her that I would stop and have relapsed when she needed me the most. She won't hate me forever right?" he asked Mrs Miller who was pottering around the room, tidying up.

"Of course not, love. You two are twin flames. You are meant to be together, Remember, love passionately and fight passionately too. You just have to make it up to her. Show her you care and are willing to go back to the Nick that we all love and care about. The Nick that I am proud to have helped raise." Nick smiled sincerely at her. The first genuine smile, he felt that he had cracked all day.

"Thank you," he said, pulling her into a warm embrace and kissing her on the cheek. "I don't know what I would do without you."

She laughed as he walked away. "Me neither, my boy. Me neither."

Nick ran outside, shouting farewell to his mother in the process and ran as fast as he could. He hoped that he knew Lillian well enough that he knew where she would be, but it was a risk. He wasn't sober enough to drive and the exercise would do him good. He needed to punish himself, just a little bit for everything that he had put his love through.

He ran through the country lanes, across the fields and slowly came to a stop at a familiar little plot of land.

"You look content," he said quietly as he laid down beside her, refusing to touch her but close enough that she could feel his body heat.

"I am," she sighed, looking up at the night sky. "Do you want to know what I've realised whilst I've been here?"

The wind whirled around them fluttering through their hair, like fingers caressing them.

Nick nodded his head and turned it towards her, watching her pale features glisten in the moonlight.

"The saddest thing about betrayal and disappointment, isn't what has caused you to feel that way, but who caused it…"

She looked at him as she pushed herself off the ground and wrapped her coat tighter around her shivering body.

Nick followed her actions and moved to follow her, before she placed her hand up onto his chest to stop him.

"I'm not living my life any more, I'm just going through the motions. I want to be happy and be there for this little one," she said, gently caressing her stomach. "But we need to be able to be happy away from each other before we are happy together."

She took a step away from him, but he reached out and grabbed her hand. "No, I don't want to miss out on anything. I want to be there for you, save you from this life. Create a better one for you both. I want to make you happy again, like I used to…" He looked down, not sure whether to step closer or not. He didn't want to push her away.

"Don't worry," Lillian said, looking at Nick and cupping his face lightly. "You were never meant to save me anyway." She stood up on her tiptoes and placed a tender kiss on his lips.

She turned around, her coat billowing around her, and walked away from him into the darkness, the only thing highlighting her path, the full moon overhead as he cried out, the most animalistic noise that he had ever heard, being ripped from his chest as he watched her retreat.

Chapter Thirty-One

Steve called his son into the dining room. "Son, we need to talk to you."

"Yes father. Is everything okay?" he asked looking at his mother's ashen face.

"Lillian turned up here last night," his mother said, looking at her teacup in front of her. She had not managed to drink any of it, and was just staring at its contents.

"Where is she? I've been trying to get hold of her all night? I know she was on a mission, which by the way we need to talk about…"

"Son, sit down," his father said seriously.

"I mean there is no way I can let her carry on just now. Wait, where is she?" Nick rambled on.

"Son, please sit down," his father repeated.

"Dad?" Nick asked, his stomach dropping when he saw his father's face.

Steve's heart dropped. His son only called him Dad when he was upset. . It was always father or his given name. Nick looked so lost. He clearly loved the girl, his soon to be daughter-in-law.

His mother came around the table and wrapped her arms around her son, pressing his head against her chest in a motherly way.

"Nick, there was an accident. Lillian arrived here in a very bad state. She was out on a mission and was attacked. Mrs Miller has been with her since she got here," his mother started.

"Attacked? Is she okay?" he started.

"Nick, I'm really sorry," his father started, "the warlock that attacked you, found out she was your partner and went after her…"

"No!" Nick shouted, "No! This can't end like this. She can't be… Where is she?"

His mother was crying, and he wrapped his arms around her tightly. The grief overtaking everything as his vision started to go black.

"I'm sorry Nick. She's upstairs, but she didn't make it," his father said, his voice cracking on the last word. "We tried to make her as comfortable as possible." Nick collapsed into his mother's arms, sobs wracking through his entire body as he clung to his mother.

"No! No! No!" Nick cried out. "No! My love! The baby!" The tears were flowing freely down his face now as his mother cradled his head against her.

"Baby?" his father asked.

Nick stood up, towering above both his parents. "Yes, baby! She was pregnant. You were going to be grandparents, but someone has taken them both from me. Why? Why did you have to do this? Why did you have to recruit her of all people? We spoke about this... I asked you. I asked you so many times and you said you would fix it." He ran from the room, leaving his shocked parents behind.

"Mrs Miller?" he shouted as he ran through the hallway. "Mrs Miller?"

She appeared from around the corner. "I'm so sorry Nick. I'm so very sorry."

"Where is she? Take me to her please? I was a dick to her and I never even got to apologise. It can't be the end. I need her more than anything. She's the only reason that I had to sober up."

He followed the little old woman through the corridors until he was outside his childhood room. He opened the door and the familiarity of it all hit him hard and then he saw her, spread out on his single bed, her black dress spilling over the sides.

"I'm so sorry my love," he cried as he walked over to her cold, pale body, placing his head gently on her stomach. The tears flowed freely.

"I'm sorry I couldn't protect you, either of you."

"Nick, my dear, I have something to tell you," Mrs Miller started.

"She was pregnant. I was going to be a daddy," he cried out. "I was going to be the best dad that I could. Better than that man down the stairs..."

"I know, my dear. I have some news about that," she started. "You cannot tell anyone about this as I'm not meant to be able to do this."

Mrs Miller waved a hand over her head and as if a cloak was being dropped from her, a woman with hair as white as his beloved stood in front of him. She looked so much like Lillian, her eyes, only made older by small laughter lines at the side and her smile was identical.

"This may be a shock to you my dear. I am Lillian's mother, Eva. Everyone thought I was dead, so I placed a charm over myself to disguise how I look. When I saw you take Lillian home to meet your parents that day, I was thrilled but terrified at the same time. I know what your father is like. I worked for him for years. I cast a spell that day to protect you both. At the moment she is in a death-like sleep. Everyone will assume she is dead so that no one else will come after her."

Nick looked at the woman in front of her and collapsed on the floor.

"She missed you so much. She would cry herself to sleep thinking about you," he cried. "Wait, she said it was cancer that took you from her."

"That's what her father said. Her father and yours, they saw my magic as a type of cancer as I developed stronger powers. They thought it was invading my cells. They thought I was weak, but the fact was I wasn't. I threatened them. It's why I had to go into hiding. To protect myself and Lillian."

Nick looked up at Lillian's mother, a light bulb going off in his head. "It makes sense now!"

"What does dear?" she asked, sitting down beside him.

"Why it didn't work when she tried to contact you. Everything seemed to be going perfectly. Her magic was exceptional, but she couldn't contact you. It was because you were here all along," Nick stated, everything falling into place in his head.

She nodded her head. "I saw her magic at work several times. The little robin she spoke about visiting her is my familiar," she said, lifting up her hand whilst the robin came flying into the room, stopping to nuzzle Nick's cheek before landing on Eva's hand. She petted its head lightly, ruffling its feathers affectionately.

Nick nodded his head in understanding. He ran his hand gently over Lillian's cheek. "I knew she couldn't be dead. I would have felt it. I would have felt our bond being broken. Like she did when I was injured. She's my soulmate, my twin flame. I would have known."

"I know," she replied, moving to wrap an arm around the broken man on the floor.

"Wait!" he exclaimed. He muttered Revelare particeps and sighed in relief as he saw his mark appear on his arm.

"Why do you keep it hidden?" Eva asked, smiling at the proof of her daughter's soulmate.

"If anyone knew, they would use it against me. They would know to hurt me, they would have to hurt her," he explained, affectionately running his fingers over the mark on his wrist.

A thought struck him and he suddenly got choked up. "What about the baby?" he croaked out, looking at her hopefully.

"The baby will keep growing. I will help look after her and keep the baby fed and healthy, you just have to keep your father away from her," she said, taking his face between her hands.

"I can do that. I can place protection spells on the room and an enchantment on Lillian to keep her hidden if need be," he said looking at his love lying still. "I'm stronger than he is now. That's why he was training us."

"Nick, you have eight months until the baby will be here and during those eight months, you will need to be able to reverse the charm I have placed on her. You are the only one that can break it due to your bond but it won't be easy. You need to not let your emotions take control which I understand will be difficult. You need to seem like you are moving on and not let others see how broken up you are about this all. Make it seem like there was some sort of mistake with you being soulmates. I know it's going to be difficult," she explained, patting his hand gently.

"I can do that. What do I need to do?" he asked, looking sincerely at her.

She sighed. "You need to kill the person that did this to her to bring her back."

Nick nodded. "Who was that? How do I find him?" he asked, anger rising within him.

Lillian's mother waved her hand over her head again, placing her Mrs Miller façade back in place. She smiled gently, a smile Nick knew all too well coming from Mrs Miller and she placed a hand on his shoulder.

"That I can help you with. There are two magical signatures attached to her death. Both of these will need to be dealt with."

Nick looked up at her hopefully, a small smile gracing his lips until he saw the sad look on her face.

"Where is he?" he asked her again.

"Nick, dear, I think they have hidden the truth from you. It wasn't this warlock they said that it was," she said, looking grimly at him, "he was just a decoy who got paid a lot to cover for them."

"Who is it?" he asked, his hands balling up into fists.

"Her father is one," she said.

Nick sighed and raked a hand through his hair. "Okay I've met him a few times. I didn't think he was practising magic any more. That's what Lillian said. He was too devastated by your death that he wouldn't do any magic."

"That's not strictly true. He was upset because he couldn't use the magic that I had been gifted and combine our magic together. Especially since the magic for the job that we do is so powerful."

Nick nodded in understanding. He was slightly confused as the man who he had met had seemed like he wouldn't hurt a fly. "Wait, who's the other then?"

"Nick, once I tell you this, there is no going back."

She knew that this was going to be hard for him to hear, but if he wanted his family back, as well as hers, she would have to tell him the truth.

223

"Tell me!" he ordered, his eyes narrowing in frustration and anger.

"Your father is the other."

His face hardened up and his eyes went cold. "I was meant to save her... Consider it done!" was all that he said, before he left the room, his coat billowing behind him.

To be continued...